IMPROVISE

SCROGGINS FAMILY SERIES - VOLUME 11

LARRY D. BLACK

TRUE IDENTITY
Copyright © 2022 Larry D. Black

All intellectual property rights are reserved. Except for brief quotations incorporated in critical articles and reviews, no part of this book may be used or reproduced by any means, graphic, electronic, or mechanical, including photocopying, recording, taping, or information storage and retrieval system, without the written permission of the author.

Media Literary Excellence
508 West 26th Street, Kearney, NE 68848
www.medialiteraryexcellence.com
1-402-819-3224

Because of the dynamic nature of the Internet, any web addresses or URLs can be changed at any time. Links in this book may have changed since it was first published, and it's possible that it's no longer valid. The opinions stated in the work are strictly those of the author. The views expressed here are those of the author and do not necessarily reflect those of the publisher. The publisher expressly disclaims any and all liability for them.

Any individuals represented in stock imagery given by copyright-free sites are the property of their respective owners. The usage of models and similar images is solely for illustrative purposes.

ISBN (Paperback): 978-1-958082-08-9
ISBN (Ebook): 978-1-958082-09-6

Printed in the United States of America

FOREWORD

This is Volume 11 about the Scroggins Family. The primary character is Sonny Scroggins, the oldest son of Lewis and Jo Scroggins whose story is in Volume 5 entitled *This Road I'm On.* This book is laced with adventure from beginning to end with a balance of romance which should keep the interest of any reader. Sonny, a scuba diver instructor and an old Vietnam helicopter pilot was the only one with credentials to rescue a friend who had been taken captive to work on a special scientific assignment. When the plans went awry, Sonny had to improvise just to stay alive.

Like all the Scroggins novels, this story is completely fiction and any identity to real people or incidents is entirely coincidental.

CHAPTER 1

A crowd was watching with concern as I swam as quickly as I could toward a victim who was apparently drowning. I could see flailing hands on the water's crest as a person surfaced from beneath the water. The closer I got, the more clearly I could see the panic in this young girl's face. As I got within about ten feet of her, she went under and failed to come back up. My arms were fatigued, but I was swimming on adrenaline. I dove beneath the surface in the murky water of Lake Eli frantically searching for what I feared was now a lifeless body. Every second was crucial. I held my breath as long as I could do so, but I finally had to go to the surface for another breath of air before diving back under the water. Finally, I saw her and swam as fast as I could toward her. When I got there, the young girl was limp and lifeless as I had expected. While I was grabbing hold of her, I could hear the sound of a motor coming our way, and I knew that a boat was coming to her aid.

When I got the girl to the surface, the boat was only a few feet away and quickly floated over to where we were. Three fishermen were in the boat, and they helped hoist the girl aboard. I climbed in immediately and began using my restoration training as I yelled for the man at the helm to head for shore. I pressed and pushed on the girl's chest while forcing air from my body into her mouth. This seemed to go on for a long time, but it was actually only a few seconds. Finally, she coughed which was the greatest sound I had heard in days. Life was coming back to her as she continued to cough and spit up water that had filled her lungs. By the time the boat got to shore, an ambulance was driving up. The paramedics quickly got her loaded and rushed her to the local hospital.

After all the excitement had diminished, the men in the boat and I introduced ourselves while several others from the crowd expressed their appreciation to me. I told them my name was Allan Scroggins, but everyone called me "Sonny."

Before I could leave the area, a local newspaper reporter showed up and wanted to interview me. He asked me who I was and where I was from. I told him my name and that I owned a scuba diving store in Norton. I also told him that I was down here checking out Lake Eli as a possible place to bring our scuba club for one of our quarterly outings. He said it was wonderful that someone with skill in saving a drowning person was in the area at just the right moment. I told him I was incredibly happy to make the rescue and that we call it "rescue and revive" or, "R & R" for short.

Finally, all the excitement was over, and the crowd and reporters were gone. It was also time for me to go as I had about sixty miles to drive before getting home.

Home for me was a double-wide modular home that was parked behind the scuba shop. It was small but big enough for an ole single bachelor like me. The shop was named *NSC*, which stood for *Norton's Scuba Club* and was located near the edge of the small east Texas town of Norton, which had a population of about 15,000 people. The primary sources of income for the citizens there were the *ETEX Lumber Mill* and the *Southern Power Company* sub-station. The primary generation plant was near Beaumont which was some

150 miles away. Several recreational lakes that provided municipal water, as well as excellent fishing, were in the vicinity. Because of the lakes nearby, there was a lot of interest in scuba diving.

Before I left the Lake Eli area, I stopped by the local hospital to check on the little girl who had almost drowned. She was in a room and doing great. The medical staff was keeping her a few hours for observation, but they all felt that she would make a full recovery with no problems. In a case like this, there was always the danger of brain damage due to the lack of blood supply. Fortunately, the doctors didn't seem to think that was the case with this little girl.

I went into her room and then introduced myself to her and her parents who were at her bedside. She said her name was Ann. I asked her what happened to cause her near-drowning. She said she was riding her jet ski when she hit something below the surface of the water that tossed her off into the lake. She was not able to swim and was not wearing a life jacket, which made her at the mercy of someone else once she was in the water. She said she was twelve years old and that she went jet skiing without her parents' knowledge. They were inside their camper taking a nap when she slipped away.

I told her I was the one who saw her flailing in the water and swam out to save her. She said she remembered some arms being around her but nothing else. She thanked me, and her parents, with tears in their eyes, couldn't thank me enough. Her mother hugged me so tightly that I thought she would crush my ribs!

Her dad also had tears in his eyes and offered to pay me money or to do anything else that could express their gratitude and appreciation. I told them I was more than happy to have done what I did, and nothing more was necessary from them. Before I left, I said to Ann, "Have you learned a lesson from this?" And she said, "Yes, Sir. I certainly have!" Her mom was hugging her tightly as I left the room.

I was home before bedtime and had a message on my telephone from Scottie, my right-hand man in the shop. He said some men from the power company stopped by and wanted to visit with me about teaching and certifying some of their employees as divers.

There was also a message from Mom wishing me a happy birthday. I had forgotten all about it being my birthday, but Mom never forgets. Even though I have three siblings, triplets I might add, Mom has a way of making each of us feel special and loved in our own way. I've heard her say a thousand times that the best thing that ever happened to her was when Lewis Scroggins came into the coffee shop where she worked and then into our lives forever.

I know I must have disappointed them some when I left my dental profession to work in a scuba-diving shop. But after four years of dental practice in the military, I realized I really didn't like it and every day I found myself dreading to go work.

Finally, I was in bed and reflecting back over the day. I was so thankful that I was able to save Ann's life. I hoped she was sincere when she said she had learned her lesson and would never again use the jet ski without her parent's permission or without wearing a life jacket. She also needed to learn to swim. I was so pleased with the way everything turned out, soon I was in a peaceful sleep.

The next morning, I was awakened by Fuzzy, my long-haired cat. She is a well-trained inside cat and probably would not fare very well if she had to live outside. Fuzzy sleeps in the laundry room, but every morning, she comes to my bedroom and jumps up on the bed and climbs on top of me as if to say, "It's time to get up." I don't need an alarm clock with Fuzzy around.

I love almost all animals as they always seem to be happy. You can really scold a dog or a cat about something, and the next day they have forgotten it and are as happy as they can be. I developed a love for animals when I was small. For a while, Mom and Dad had a small farm in East Texas where we had a few pets, but my Uncle Ben had cows and horses as he operated a dairy before being elected county sheriff.

Once Fuzzy had me up, I was soon dressed and on the way to the scuba store. I stopped at a convenience store and grabbed a dozen donuts for breakfast. Mom would say that was not a nutritious breakfast, but they sure do taste good! Scottie was already at the store and was glad to see the bag of donuts.

He had the coffee pot going, and the smell of fresh coffee was a pleasant aroma as I walked in. There were a few minutes before time to open the shop, so we talked about what the men from the power plant wanted as we downed the donuts and coffee.

Scottie said they have six men who need to be certified for underwater diving. It seems the dam for the water reservoir has to be inspected annually, and they figure it would be cheaper to have their own divers than to contract the work out to another company. Scottie said they wanted to talk with me about the training and were supposed to come by, first thing this morning.

Shortly after the shop was opened, two men driving a truck from the power company came in. I introduced myself, and we went into my office. They said they understood that I was a licensed scuba-diving instructor who was qualified to train and certify divers. I told them they were correct, and I asked what they specifically wanted me to do.

They repeated what Scottie had said about having six men who needed to be certified to dive and make repairs underwater, if needed, to the dam on the discharge lake for *S.E.T. Power Company*. "We need these men to not only be able to dive some forty-to-sixty feet but also be able to make repairs if needed, which would include welding. Can you teach them?"

I told him I could and asked if the men had any experience in diving.

"No experience at all. They have never done any diving. But, all of them can swim and are young and very athletic. I feel that diving would come naturally to them."

Immediately, I knew this was going to be a challenge. I told the men that it would take up to six months for the training and certification to be completed and that it would take even longer if the classes were interrupted for some reason. I told them my fee, and they never blinked an eye as they were good with my terms.

I told them I could start next week with a class on Tuesday and Thursday evenings here at the shop after it was closed for the day. This time schedule, however, would create a problem for the men. Even though a sub-station is here in Norton, the primary plant where the men work is about 150 miles away and getting them here for evening classes would be difficult week after week.

So they asked if I would be willing to drive to Beaumont and conduct the classes there. Then, they added that they would pay for all of my expenses, including mileage, overnight lodging, and meals. I told them I could drive there for the first few weeks as we would be doing classroom training, but at some point, we would have to get into the water. They asked if a swimming pool would suffice, and I told them it would in the beginning but not when we got farther into the training. They agreed to locate a pool that we could use in the beginning. We shook hands and they left.

There were no customers in the shop when the men left, so I called Scottie into the office and we discussed the lucrative arrangement I had just made. I asked if he could pull together the material I used when I taught classes and make about ten copies of each page. That would be enough for the students plus a few extras.

While we were talking about the class, I received a telephone call from Dad. He said Mom had been rushed to the Regional Hospital in Wichita Falls with what they feared was a heart attack. I was stunned, to say the least, and told Dad that I'd be there as soon as I could get there.

Scottie knew, by my end of the conversation, as well as my demeanor, that something was wrong. I told him what Dad had said and asked if he could manage the shop for a few days as I needed to go be with my family. He was totally in agreement and was willing to help in any way that he could. I was very lucky to have him as a friend as well as an employee.

A customer came into the shop, and as Scottie went to wait on him, he gave me a thumbs-up while I walked out the back door. I hurriedly packed a few things and put ample food in an automatic feeder for Fuzzy. I didn't have to worry about water as she drank from the toilet bowl. Within fifteen minutes, I was on the road.

While pushing the speed limit, I kept thinking about Mom and what she meant to me. I remember how excited she was when she told me about Lewis and how she hoped someday he would be my stepdad. I was excited because of her excitement.

I really don't remember very much about my biological dad other than he had a dark mustache. I remember going to his funeral and wondering why so many people were crying. I remember Mom taking me by the hand as we walked from the graveyard back to the car. Mom never seemed happy again until Lewis, known to me now as Dad, became part of our lives. I immediately called him "Dad" and he legally adopted me soon after they were married.

My thoughts were interrupted by a school bus stopping to let some children off. That reminded me of my school days and how Mom and Dad were always at my ballgames or anything else I was involved in. Mom was always my number-one fan. I could hear her yelling above everyone else. I remembered glancing up into the stands and seeing Dad trying to calm her down.

Then there was the time when the triplets were born. She had a glow on her face like an angel from heaven. I could tell that she was concerned that I might be jealous of them when she brought them home, but I adored all three of them from the first time I saw them. I enjoyed being the "big brother" and helping in every way I could, such as bringing diapers to Mom or even rocking one of them to sleep. They were all grown up now and for a while, we had remained a very close-knit family. But in the past few years, we seemed to have drifted apart and hadn't gotten together like we once did.

Now there was a real concern that Mom might be dying. It just can't be! Even though I was a grown man, my life would be in such shambles without Mom. I prayed fervently that God would spare her life. While I was not living as spiritually as I knew I should, I still had a deep faith in the power of prayer and asked God for divine intervention in making Mom well.

As I approached Dallas, the traffic was heavier which demanded my full attention. It seemed like I would never get across town, but I eventually did. I was getting hungry but hated to stop. Those doughnuts were long gone out of my stomach. I grabbed a package of peanuts and a Pepsi at the gas station which I hoped would hold me over. I smiled to myself as I again thought Mom would say this wasn't nutritious.

Finally, just before dark, I arrived at the hospital in Wichita Falls. I then asked the lady at the front desk where Jo Scroggins was, and I was told where to go. As I was walking down the hall toward her room, I heard someone call my name. I stopped and whirled around to see my brother, Kevin. I could tell by the look on his face that he was worried.

"How's Mom and where is Dad?" I asked apprehensively.

CHAPTER 2

Kevin said Mom was in surgery and Dad was in the waiting room where he could speak with the surgeon when he comes out. He said he had come down to the vending machines for a snack and drink when he saw me walking down the hall.

I was confused and asked why there was surgery for a heart attack. Kevin replied that she didn't have a heart attack but had a gall bladder attack. He said the symptoms are very similar, and the doctors thought it was her heart until they did some testing. He said she had been in surgery for almost two hours, and that hopefully, they would be finished soon.

We talked as we walked to where Dad was. As we approached the waiting room, I could see Dad talking with the doctor. Quickly Kevin and I rushed over to hear what he had to say, and when Dad saw me, he reached out and embraced me and introduced me to the doctor.

The doctor looked at Kevin and me and said, "I was just telling your dad that all went well and that your mom should be just fine. There was a little excessive bleeding early on. But when we got that under control, everything else was textbook perfect."

Then, he shifted his attention from us back to Dad and said, "Chaplain, we got to her just in time. I've never seen a gall bladder in worse shape. It looked as though it could have ruptured at any time, and if it had, it would have been fatal for sure. But thankfully, that didn't happen, and I expect a full recovery."

"When can we see her?" Kevin asked.

"She is in the recovery room and should be back in her room in about an hour. You can wait for her there. She will still be a little groggy at first."

"Thank you, Doctor," Dad said.

"You are very welcome," the doctor replied as he turned to walk away.

I realized now how hungry I was and told Dad and Kevin that I was going to get a snack. They went along with me, and after a while, we made it up to Mom's room and waited.

While we waited, Dad told us how he was enjoying spending his days after retiring as the Air Force Chaplain, and I told them about the men from the power plant wanting me to teach their employees to dive. Kevin shared some things that he was doing as a forest ranger s well. Then Dad said he had almost forgotten to tell me that Ron Cunningham stopped by his house a couple of days ago and wanted to see me. I haven't seen Ron since high school and wondered why he wanted to see me. I told Dad that I would try to hook up with him before I leave town.

While we were visiting, the door was pushed open and Mom was rolled into the room. She was awake and was glad to see us. Dad told her about the surgery and that after a few days, she should be as good as new. After we visited for a few minutes, Dad insisted that I go to their house for a good night's sleep as he planned to spend the night here with Mom. I was tired and the offer sounded good to me, so I said good-night. Soon, Kevin and I left the hospital.

The next morning, when I returned, Mom was sitting up in bed with her make-up on and had just finished eating breakfast. She said the nurse would be having her walk some a little later in the day. While I was there, the doctor came in and looked at her incision and told us that everything looked good.

Since all was looking good, I told Mom and Dad that I really needed to get back home, so I said goodbye and left. Before leaving town, I went by Ron Cunningham's parents' house to get some contact information for him. His mother was glad to see me and wanted me to stay for some coffee and cake, but I graciously declined her offer. She gave me Ron's telephone number and his address in Ft. Worth. She said she knew he had gone by Mom and Dad's house the last time he was in town in hopes that I might be there, but she had no idea why he wanted to see me.

After I left Mrs. Cunningham's house, I stopped at a telephone booth and called Ron. To my surprise, he was home and seemed glad that I called. He said he needed to talk with me and asked if I could possibly come by to see him on my way back home. I told him I could and asked what was going on. He said we would talk when we got together, and after giving me directions to his house, he hung up.

I was curious, to say the least, as I wondered what in the world Ron could possibly want from me. After a couple of hours, I was at his house. He invited me inside and offered me a glass of iced tea. We then went out to sit on his covered patio. I quickly asked him what he had on his mind. He surprised me by asking if I still flew helicopters.

During the Vietnam War, I was a Cobra Helicopter Pilot and flew rescue missions. If soldiers were wounded behind enemy lines, rescue pilots would fly in and attempt to rescue them. These were extremely dangerous assignments, and more than 50 percent of rescue pilots were shot down themselves.

I was shot down twice, but I had the good fortune of being able to guide my chopper back to friendly territory each time before crashing. The last time I was shot down, I sustained a broken back which led to me being shipped back home. After several back surgeries, I regained the use of my legs, and swimming was recommended as good therapy which evolved into my scuba diving. I really don't know how many hours of flying time I logged, but it was a lot, to say the least. Once I recovered from the back injury I started practicing dentistry which I soon realized I didn't like.

I told Ron that I hadn't flown in years and that I was now a scuba diver instructor. "Why do you ask?" I quizzed.

"Sonny, your parents had told me that you are a scuba diver which is why I wanted to talk with you. I need to tell you something in confidence. If word gets out about this conversation, then both of our lives will be in danger."

On hearing that, I became very nervous. But Ron was a friend, and if he needed help, at least I could listen to what he had to say. "Go on," I said.

He told me that he was working for a chemical company that had a military top-secret assignment. He said they were working on developing a chemical of mass destruction. That was disturbing enough, but he then added, "Tim, our top scientist, is missing. We can't release this information to the authorities since it is classified and the government disavows any knowledge of this project or his whereabouts."

"I really hate to hear about this," I replied. "But what does it have to do with me?" I asked.

"I want you to try to find and rescue him."

"What? I can't do that!"

"Sonny, you are the only one who can! I need someone with both helicopter and diving experience. You are the only person I know who can do both."

I told him that I didn't have a helicopter, nor did I even know where I could get one. He assured me that he would take care of that part.

My next objection was that I didn't know where to begin to start looking for Tim nor did I even know what he looked like and wouldn't know him if I found him. At once, Ron gave me a picture of him and said he guessed him to be in Yemen.

"Yemen? What makes you think he is in Yemen?

Ron explained that the classified assignment they were working on was for the military, but it wasn't for our military — it was for the Republic of Omen. He said Omen was preparing themselves for military attacks from their neighboring enemy, Yemen. "Somehow, I think someone in Yemen found out about our project and took Tim for his in-depth knowledge of this research. Exactly where he is, I don't know. But I believe he is in Yemen which has a lot of water and desert. Sonny, I need your services. I can arrange to pay you well for your effort plus get you whatever supplies you need."

"Ron, you're my friend, but I don't think I'm your man. I'm sorry, but you need to get someone else."

"Sonny, there is no one else I can get that I trust!"

"I'm sorry, Ron, but my answer is no."

Ron said he understood and asked that I keep this conversation in confidence, and I assured him that I would.

All the way back to Norton, I thought about what Ron had shared with me. I knew that I shouldn't get involved in this as it was none of my business, not to mention the danger. Besides, I have the scuba shop to manage and really couldn't afford to be gone for an extended period of time. Plus, to complicate matters, I wouldn't be able to tell Scottie where I was going or why I was leaving. I just really couldn't do this. Dad taught me what his dad had taught him and that is to "always think it through" before making a major decision.

When I arrived back at the shop, Scottie had things under control, as I expected, and he immediately wanted to know about my mother. I told him that it wasn't her heart as we first thought but that it was her gall bladder, which was removed, and that she was recovering fine. He was glad to hear that news and then told me all that happened in the shop while I was gone. He also had all the class material ready for me to begin teaching next week.

Time passed, and it was soon time for my first scuba class with the six men from *S.E.T.P.C.* I drove down to Beaumont and found the training building for the power company without any difficulty. I arrived a few minutes early which gave me time to get everything out of the car and into the classroom without any distractions. As I was positioning the last packet of material on the table where the men would be sitting, they all came in at the same time.

I introduced myself to them and told them I was a certified PADI, which meant *Professional Association of Divers Instructor.* They, in turn, told me their names and a little about themselves. Then I asked them if they knew what the term "scuba" meant as they were all seeking to become scuba divers. None of them did.

I informed them that "scuba" was an acronym for *'Self Contained Underwater Breathing Apparatus.'* "As the name implies, and as you all know, you will be learning how to use self-contained equipment that will allow you to breathe underwater. Since we were not born to be like fish, we need some additional help – thus scuba equipment."

Then I asked them if they could name some equipment that they would need in order to breathe underwater. They all had seen enough movies that they knew they would need a tank of air, a mask, fins, and an air hose that goes from the air tank to their mouth. I commended them for their answers and told them we would learn a few more things.

I gave them some general information that they would need to know. I said, "First of all, you must always dive with a partner and never try to do it solo. As a new diver, you will require more air than you will after you become an experienced diver. You mentioned that you would need a tank of air, and perhaps you are wondering if the tank will be heavy.

It will seem heavy before you get into the water, but once you begin the dive, it doesn't seem heavy at all, and we will even add some weights to hold it down. You don't necessarily need to be an Olympic swimmer to be a good diver, but you can't be afraid of the water, and you must demonstrate to me your ability to swim continuously for 200 yards and float for 10 minutes, both without aids.

Another thing you need to remember is that your ears will "stop up" much like when riding on an airplane. You will need to blow frequently to clear them, and some people have actually had their eardrums burst from the pressure of the water.

Many people find it hard to get back onto the boat when they re-surface, so don't be afraid to ask for help if you need it. One last thing is that you will be the exception if you aren't frightened the first time you dive. Most everyone must give themselves a pep talk and tell themselves that they will be fine and that there are plenty of people around to help if they encounter any trouble. We will talk more along these lines in future classes. Be sure to ask any questions that you might have. Remember, there is no such thing as a dumb question."

"I went on to explain to them that in order to complete their PADI Open Water Diver certification, they must complete five confined water dives, five academic sessions, and four open water dives. "The confined water dives are generally done in a swimming pool with clear, shallow water. Most people think those first dives in a swimming pool are harder than the deep-water dives. During these sessions, you will learn how to do basic diving skills such as mask clearing, regulator clearing, and air management. However, the most basic prerequisite to becoming a qualified scuba diver is to feel comfortable in the water."

I continued with, "The academic sessions involve viewing videotapes, reading the manual I've handed out to you, answering a series of questions based on the videos and readings, and successfully passing quizzes that verify your understanding of the material. Now I know you do not like to hear the word *quizzes or tests*, but they are a necessary evil. By the time you take a quiz, you will be prepared for the questions and there will not be any trick questions. Diving safely requires you to have a basic understanding of dive physics and physiology. You will be asked to apply that knowledge in the pool, so it's important to learn the academic material. Fortunately, most of this work can be done independently in the comfort of your home. We always stress "safety first." You will not be allowed to dive until we are satisfied that you know all of the safety rules."

"When you have completed Phase 1, which is the confined water dives and classroom studies, we will move on to open-water dives. That is what most people look forward to. As previously stated, there will be four of these dives, and they will be done in the company discharge lake. In these dives, you will demonstrate the skills you've learned for the kind of conditions you will be diving in. I limit this type of dives to only two a day, which means it will take two days to complete this session. When you're finished, you will be issued a certification card with your picture on it, proving that you are a certified diver!

Altogether, your certification training will probably take about thirty-five to forty hours of your time. After you are certified, then we will advance to underwater welding techniques."

"As I understand it, your reason for becoming a certified diver is so you can do what is required for your job. However, there is nothing that would stop you from going to the Caribbean on a vacation and diving down to the bottom of the ocean just for fun. I have done that, and there is no way you can imagine, or that I can describe, the beauty you will see on the ocean floor. I encourage all of you to do that at least once, and I suspect you will want to return again and again."

"Any questions?"

"Will my certification expire every year?" one student asked.

"No. As an 'Open Water Diver', your certification is good for life and will not expire. However, if you do not actively participate in scuba for an extended period of time, it's a good idea to take the PADI Scuba Review to brush up on your skills. Any other questions?"

There were none, so we began our first lesson. We talked about additional equipment with which they needed to familiarize themselves. We discussed the purpose of each item, and I finally closed the session by explaining one major concern for divers which was the 'quality vision.'

"Much of being in the underwater world requires good vision, and glasses are not a good solution because they generally don't fit or attach easily to the inside of a dive mask. Soft or gas permeable contacts work as well underwater as they do on land and many divers use them successfully." When the class came to an end, I stressed again the importance of safety and common sense, and the students seemed to be excited and could hardly wait to get into the water. Each one told me how much he had enjoyed the class and was looking forward to the next meeting. I felt good about the class also.

After class was dismissed and as I was driving back to Norton, my thoughts kept drifting back to Ron Cunningham and his predicament. For some reason, I just couldn't shake it. I decided that tomorrow I would give him another call to discuss another meeting.

The next morning, Fuzzy woke me up early, as usual, and after my first cup of coffee, I called Ron. Someone else answered and I asked to speak to Ron. The unfamiliar voice said, "Haven't you heard?"

CHAPTER 3

Frantically I asked what had happened. At first, she didn't want to talk to me, but I finally assured her that Ron and I were long-time friends. She then said that she was an employee where Ron worked and that he had failed to report to work for two days. The coworkers were concerned and went to his house to check on him. When they got there, the house was a bloody mess and a severed hand was on the kitchen table with a note saying, "Stay out of other people's business or more will happen!"

I was stunned and didn't say a word for several seconds. Then I heard the lady's voice saying, "Sir, are you there? Are you there, sir?"

"Ah yes ….. I'm here. What you told me just took my breath away for a second. I'm sorry. My name is Sonny Scroggins, and Ron and I were high school buddies. Do you have any idea what happened?"

"No, sir, we don't. The FBI agents are here trying to make some sense of everything."

"Is Ron alive?" I asked, fearful of the answer.

"Mr. Scroggins, we just don't know. A body hasn't been found here."

Just before I hung up the phone, I asked her name and she said, "Kali Huff." I thanked her for the information and then hung up the phone. I just sat there almost in a trance. I was wondering if agents from Yemen had done that, and then I wondered if they knew about my conversation with Ron. I wondered if his house had been bugged and if our conversation was recorded. I decided I had better keep a watch over my shoulder and pay close attention to my surroundings just as a precaution.

Finally, I made my way to the shop. The first thing Scottie said was, "What happened to you? You look like you just lost your best friend!"

"I may have," I replied.

"Hey, man. What's wrong?"

"I'm not sure I can, or should, tell you."

"Come on, man. You know that you can trust me."

I told him that it wasn't a matter of trust but rather it was a matter of safety. Now, this really aroused his curiosity. Finally, I broke down and told him the whole story and that I didn't know what I should do. Deep down, I felt that Ron had been apprehended just like Tim and that I should try to rescue both of them. Our government certainly won't do anything as it has no knowledge of their mission. Likewise, our military is not involved in the matter.

I turned to Scottie for advice. If I did attempt a rescue mission, how would I do it? What kind of plan could I have, and how would I ever find them? "Scottie, where could I even start?"

Scottie didn't have any ideas better than mine, but he did suggest that I could start by nosing around the company where Ron worked. For now, that sounded like the most logical thing to do. I started making plans to go back to Ft. Worth.

As we were talking, I remembered my scuba class. I asked Scottie if he would teach the classes for me, and hopefully, I would be back by the time the swimming sessions began. He was certainly capable of teaching the material and instructing the students in the use of the equipment. He agreed but said it would mean closing the shop early on the class days, but I had no problem with that.

I left the shop and headed for Ft. Worth. On the way, I kept thinking about what I was going to say or what I was going to do because I was not supposed to know anything about the project, nor did I know who did or did not know about the contract within the company. I figured I would begin by talking to Kali and play it by ear from there.

The drive was pleasant as the traffic was light and the countryside was beautiful, but the closer I got to the Dallas-Ft. Worth region, the heavier the traffic became. When I was about twenty miles from Ft. Worth, it hit me like a brick wall that I didn't know the name of the chemical company where Ron worked and certainly didn't know where it was! So I was getting closer and closer to someplace that I knew not where. What was I to do?

I decided to go to Ron's house in hopes that someone might be there who could tell me where to go. When I arrived at his house, there was no one to be seen. I could not even arouse any neighbors. Finally, I decided to call Scottie and asked him to call my dad to see if he could call Ron's mom and find out the name of the company where Ron worked. I gave Scottie my phone booth number and told him that I'd stay here waiting for him to call back.

While waiting, I walked over to the nearby gas station and bought a Pepsi and a Baby Ruth candy bar. About fifteen minutes later, Scottie called and said the name of the company was *ChemTec*. I looked through the telephone book and found it was located on 21st Street. I thanked Scottie for his help and then went back over to the gas station and asked for directions to 21st Street. Finally, I made it to the right location. Before getting out of the car, I took a deep breath and said a prayer asking for wisdom and guidance.

Once inside, I asked the security guard at the front desk for Kali Huff. He wanted to know who was calling and recorded my driver license's number before calling her. Soon, a beautiful blonde walked into the lobby and over to me and said, "Are you Sonny Scroggins?"

"I am, and you must be Kali."

She got me a visitor's badge and escorted me to her office. She was a manager in Human Resources which would explain why she was at Ron's house the other day. Once we were in her office, she immediately wanted to know why I was there. I told her again that Ron and I were good friends and that I was concerned about him after our phone conversation. I asked if they had learned anything since we had talked.

She said all the investigation had been turned over to the FBI, and they had not given them any new information. I asked if Ron's mother had been notified. She said that as far as she knew, she was not. They didn't want to notify the next of kin without sufficient evidence.

While we were talking, I noticed that she was not wearing a wedding band, so I assumed that meant she was not married. For some reason, that pleased me. I also noticed that there were no family pictures in her office of children or what appeared to be a significant other. I could not imagine someone as gorgeous as she not having someone in her life, but I dared not approach that matter at this time.

I asked if I could speak with Ron's supervisor, but she said I could not because Ron was working on a classified project and I did not have the proper credentials to discuss any matter with his management.

I then asked her if she could recommend a good place to eat as I was new to this area and didn't know where to go. She recommended a Mexican restaurant about two blocks down on 21st street.

After that, she quizzed me a little bit about my past, as I'm sure it seemed odd to her that I would show up like I did and ask the questions that I was asking. I told her where I lived and that I owned a scuba diving shop, which sparked a mutual conversation as she loved to go the lakes and swim and water ski.

Finally, I left and told her that I'd try the restaurant later in the evening and asked if she would like to join me there. She thanked me but politely declined the invitation.

I left with the feeling that I hadn't accomplished very much other than I learned that the place was under heavy security and surveillance. But I needed to find out something about the project Ron was working on if I was going to plan a rescue mission!

Later that day, I made my way to the Mexican restaurant that Kali recommended. As I was eating, I decided I needed to enlist the services of my cousin, Robert, a private investigator. He lives in East Texas which is a few hours away. Tomorrow, I will head that way.

Just as I was finishing my meal, Kali walked up to my table and asked if she could join me. Naturally, I welcomed her company. She said she had hoped to catch me here because after I left the company earlier, they received some information from the forensic lab. She said, "The bloody hand that was found was not Ron's! They haven't determined whose it was, but they know it wasn't Ron's, so it must have been a set-up. However, they did find some blood that matched Ron's, so the conclusion was that there must have been a struggle and Ron was bleeding at some point."

I thanked her for the information and was dying to ask her some more questions, but I wasn't sure how much I should say. Was she part of the development team, or was she merely in human recourses with no knowledge of what was being developed? I thought I'd test the water and ask about Tim.

"The last time I visited with Ron, he mentioned having a co-worker named Tim. Do you think I could speak with him?"

She seemed a little shocked at that question and finally said, "He's out of town right now, and I'm not sure when he will be back. Do you know Tim?"

I told her that I really didn't know him personally. I just remembered Ron mentioning his name. From there the conversation changed to lighter things. She told me that she grew up in central Texas on a small farm and had two brothers. She was a cheerleader in high school. She was married, but six months into their marriage, her husband was killed in a car/train crash, and since then she had been engulfed in her work. She said this was the closest thing to a social outing she had done since his death almost two years ago.

Intermingled in the conversation, I told her about me and some of my helicopter experiences. We talked about life on a farm which led me to talk about East Texas and Uncle Ben and Uncle Pete. She said I was fortunate to have a close-knit, loving family because she was not very close to her brothers.

"In fact," she said "I don't even know where one of them is. No one has heard from him in years. The last time we heard, he was in Chicago."

Finally, it was time to go, and we walked out of the restaurant together. I escorted her to her car and told her that I had very much enjoyed our time together. She returned the sentiment, and then we parted ways.

The next morning, I drove down to East Texas to see Robert. I went to his investigative office and first saw his wife, Janet. As always, she was bubbling over with personality and was excited to see me. She said Robert was away for a few minutes but that he would be back soon. Instead of waiting, I told her I'd come back after I went by to see Uncle Ben.

When I got to the sheriff's office, I saw Uncle Ben at the coffee pot with his back to me. "Imagine that!" I said. "Ben Scroggins drinking coffee!"

Immediately, he turned, and when he saw me, he said, "Sonny! What brings you into this neck of the woods?"

I told him that I came down to visit with Robert and wanted to stop by to say hello. Uncle Ben was just as glad to see me as Janet had been. He invited me into his office, and with a cup of coffee, he told me all about my aunts, uncles, and cousins. I, in turn, told him about Mom's surgery.

I wanted to discuss my real purpose for being here but wasn't sure if I should. The more people I get involved, the more their lives might be in danger. But before I left, I did tell him that I met a girl named Kali Huff and asked if he would do a background check on her for me. He smiled and said that he'd be glad to do so.

I headed back to Robert's office, and just as I got there, he was walking up with a small sack in his hand from the local hardware store. When he saw me, he called out my name. Like Uncle Ben, he wanted to know why I was in town. He hadn't been inside his office yet, so when we walked in together, Janet said, "Well, I see you two got together without my help!"

Once we were in Robert's office, I told him my situation and how I felt I needed to try to rescue Tim, and now, most likely Ron also. But I needed more information. I, at least, needed to know Tim's last name. I also needed to know who within the company I could trust to discuss this mission and how I could obtain the necessary funding.

Robert tried to talk me out of getting involved, but I knew within my heart that I must do this for Ron's sake. He smiled as he reminded me what we had always been taught by our dads, and we in unison said, "always think it through."

When Robert realized that my mind was made up, we began to work on a plan to get some information from ChemTec. Robert said he first needed to do some background checks on the company and any employees whose names might surface. I told him about the tight security, but that didn't seem to bother him very much. He told me that it might take a couple of days before he knew anything, and after that, we'd put together a game plan.

I told Robert about asking Uncle Ben to do a background check on Kali and maybe she might be our inside person since she would have access to all personnel files. Robert's comment was, "Maybe. We'll wait and see."

After I left, I went back by Uncle Ben's, and he told me that there was no criminal record at all on Kali Huff. He said she was as clean as a new button. That was really good news to me. Uncle Ben insisted that I stay for lunch and said Aunt Mary Ann would be disappointed if I didn't. No one could turn down an invitation like that, so I agreed to have lunch with them. It was delightful to see Aunt Mary Ann, and as usual, she had a great meal prepared. The orphanage had really grown since I was there last with several new buildings added.

After lunch, I headed back down to Norton to wait until I heard from Robert. When I got there, I briefed Scottie on what I had learned, including the dinner conversation I had with Kali.

Several days passed before Robert called and asked if I could come to his office. I agreed to be there the next morning. When I arrived, Robert, Janet and I met together in his office. He said that ChemTec was a legitimate independent company that did all kinds of chemical research ranging from alternative fuel, medicine, and military reconnaissance. They have about 150 to 200 employees with about 60 percent of them having D.O.D. (Department of Defense) secret or top-secret clearances.

Then Robert outlined a plan. He said that he and Janet planned to go there and pose as D.O.D. auditors to check to see that their files were in order. That could, at least, get some names and hopefully contracts that they were working on. It would take a few days for them to have identification and credentials made along with a formal letter mailed to HR informing them of their coming.

"What can I do to help?" I asked.

"Nothing just yet other than maybe spending some time with Kali."

I smiled and said it was a tough assignment, but someone had to do it. Then I left and headed to Ft. Worth. I stopped at Chem Tec and invited Kali to dinner, and after a brief pause, she accepted. We agreed to meet at a Chinese restaurant that she recommended, and then I left.

That evening at dinner, the conversation flowed easily as much of it was about scuba diving. She said she had never done that but would love to become certified so she could. She said she wanted to go to the Caribbean and see all the beautiful things at the bottom of the ocean. I thought to myself that I would love for us to go together to do that, but I merely told her that it would be fun to do so.

Finally, I worked the conversation around to Ron, and she said they had heard nothing from the investigation team, which she thought was a little strange. I agreed and suggested that maybe there was more to what happened than they wanted us to know. To my surprise, she agreed and said, "There have been a lot of strange things happening lately."

I wanted to quiz her more but decided not to push my luck. I'd let her tell me at her own pace what she wanted me to know. So, I asked, "Do you feel threatened?"

She said she didn't, but others might. Then she told me about Tim's disappearance and now Ron's. I asked if she thought there was a connection between the two, and she said the only thing she knew that they had in common was their work contract. Thus far, she hadn't told me anything that I didn't already know, but at least she was talking.

"Do you know what they were working on?" I asked.

"No, not really. I know it was a classified program and everything was done behind closed doors."

I wanted so badly to tell her of my plans, but I wasn't sure this was the time. While I felt I could trust her, I still had to be cautious. "What is Tim's last name?" I asked.

"Huggins. His name is Tim Huggins."

"Does he have a family?"

"Yes, he has a wife and three children. They have been told he is on an assignment out of town." As she talked, her blue eyes filled with tears. I could see the compassion she had for that family.

Finally, I broke down and told her of my mission. I told her how Ron had contacted me to try to find and rescue Tim, but then he disappeared before I could get any information that could help me with this mission. She seemed shocked at what I was telling her, but after what I said had soaked in, she seemed more than willing to help. I reinforced to her the urgency of keeping all this a secret because we didn't know who we could trust, but to be assured that there was an informant somewhere inside ChemTec.

Later, we went our separate ways, and I felt good about our conversation, but at the same time a little concerned. If she was the informant, then I'd played right into her hands. If she wasn't the informant, which I chose to believe, then I may have endangered her life.

Two days later, Robert called and said, "Everything is ready. We make our move on Monday."

CHAPTER 4

Saturday night, before I went to bed, I packed a few things as I planned to drive up to Robert's after church services tomorrow so I could be ready first thing on Monday to help with the investigation of ChemTec. During the night, I was tossing and turning with Ron on my mind when my phone rang. I was surprised that anyone would call me in the middle of the night. But when I answered, a muffled voice said "Can't talk. With friend. Grand Canyon." and hung up.

I sat on the side of the bed with the phone still in my hand. What in the world was that all about? Was that Ron trying to let me know that he and Tim were being held hostage in the Grand Canyon? Was the call a hoax to try to get me to think it was Ron? Who even knew that I was aware that Tim was missing? Maybe the "friend" mentioned in the call wasn't referring to Tim at all! Now, what do I do?

If that was a legitimate call, then perhaps Ron was with Tim and they weren't in Yemen as we had been led to believe, but they were in the Grand Canyon. Did someone know of our conversation and want to throw me off the trail? Could it possibly be Kali who was setting me up? Maybe I made a mistake confiding in her, but I really didn't tell her very much.

She doesn't know anything about Robert and Janet and their plans to pretend to be auditors. All she knows is that I was asked to try to find and rescue Tim, and now possibly Ron as well. The only reason I told her anything is because I needed to know Tim's last name. Was that enough to justify her misleading me? It didn't sound like a women's voice on the phone.

Needless to say, I couldn't go back to sleep, so I just got up early and decided to head on up to Robert's. I would be there in plenty of time to attend worship services with him and Janet and their kids. It would be nice to worship with a lot of the Scroggins Family members.

That afternoon, after having dinner with Uncle Ben and Aunt Mary Ann, I had a chance to tell Robert about the phone call. He was as bewildered about it as I was, and he also said there would most likely be more calls — especially if I was getting close to the truth. I agreed and wondered what would happen if calls were made and I wasn't home to take them. I had read that visionaries seemed to think that technology was really expanding and before too many years, people would have a cell phone to carry around with them and could receive or send calls from wherever they were. I find it hard to believe that will ever happen, but it would certainly be nice if it did.

We agreed to proceed with the investigation at ChemTec, and while Robert and Janet were in Ft. Worth, I would try to find out how I could get access to a helicopter so I could check out the Grand Canyon. I know some tourist flights go into the canyon, but I wondered if an individual could rent a chopper. I couldn't seem to get that phone call out of my head! And I had no way of knowing if it was legit or from Ron. Maybe someone had dialed the wrong number and it wasn't even meant for me!

Monday morning, Robert and Janet left early to drive to Ft. Worth. They looked "official" with nametags, briefcases, official-looking letterheads on stationery, and a fake letter of authorization from the Secretary of State. Since arrangements had already been made with ChemTec for their audit visit, there shouldn't be any problem for them to get access to the files.

While they were gone, I stayed in Robert's office and used the phone to do helicopter research. I wasn't having any luck. There were a few chartered flights into the canyon, but they provided their own pilot and flew only to the tourist sites. That was discouraging so I decided to take another approach.

I called several helicopter instructors who were located near the Grand Canyon and told them I was a helicopter pilot from many years ago and wanted to get re-certified on a rotorcraft. I learned that I would need to take about ten hours of classroom refresher instruction, fifteen hours of dual flight time, as well as twenty hours of solo flight time. After that, I had to pass a written exam. All of that would probably take about six weeks before I would be eligible to fly solo. So, for about six weeks of preliminary training, I could have twenty hours of helicopter use for myself. This sounded like a good plan to me except for the $2,500 fee. Where could I come up with that kind of money? Also, if my buddy Ron was in danger, I didn't have six weeks to wait to try to rescue him.

After lunch, I walked down to the library and looked at some maps of the Grand Canyon. I was amazed at the gigantic size! The canyon covers almost 2,000 surface square miles without counting the height of the peaks with all the hiding places they could provide. A hostage could be hidden in one of those caves or crevices and never be found. I realized finding Ron would be like finding a needle in a haystack. Now I wasn't so sure that flying a helicopter through the canyon would do anything except cost me a lot of money. Plus, I didn't even know if that call came from Ron. He may be on a nice vacation with his girlfriend somewhere in the Caribbean while I am agonizing about trying to rescue him!

I sat in the library chair almost in a daze. Trying to find and rescue someone in that place would be a massive undertaking, plus I wasn't sure the telephone call was legitimate. So why did I feel such an overwhelming urge to try to investigate?

After a few hours at the library, I made my way back to Robert's office to wait for their return. While I was there, Uncle Ben stopped by to see how things were going. I assumed Robert had mentioned the case to him, so I told him about my strange telephone call and how I was discouraged when I realized how big that canyon is.

He quizzed me a little which made me now think he didn't know what was going on. So, I felt compelled to bring him into the mix. I told him the entire story from the beginning and how I was now unsure which way to turn. He offered another idea. He suggested that perhaps my cousin Terry, the Texas Game Warden, might have some contacts that could make arrangements for a heli-copter. Uncle Ben said that game wardens use them often in their line of work. I thought that was a good idea, so after he left, I called Terry and set up a time to get with him later in the evening. He agreed to come by Robert's house at about 6:30.

Just after I hung up the phone, Robert and Janet came in. "How did it go?" I eagerly asked.

"Great!" Robert said. He said the staff was very cooperative and never suspected that they weren't the "real deal." He said they were able to look at all the personnel records, and with the small camera concealed in Janet's ring, they snapped pictures of every person's file that was employed at the chemistry lab.

He said, "When we get the film developed, we can begin our study and background checks. We did find out that Tim's last name is indeed Huggins and that he was working on a program with a code name "Hot Plate." Beyond that, we found out nothing about the program other than it is behind closed doors."

With a grin, he added, "But we found out which doors they are! And that is a start."

"Did you find out anything about Kali Huff?" I asked with special interest.

"No, not really. But it was noted in the comment section of her job application that she was involved in an organized march protesting the Vietnam War during the late 1960s."

I thought to myself that happened some fifteen years ago, and a lot of people had bad feelings toward that war. Apparently, she was not arrested since Uncle Ben found no criminal record against her when he did his background search. I was hoping that she was being truthful with me and had no part in the kidnapping.

Robert asked me to stay another night with them, which I agreed to do. When we got to their house, I gave Scottie a call to tell him I would be a day later coming home. He was very glad I called as he didn't know how to contact me, and he said that some girl called the store asking for me.

I gave him Robert's telephone number and asked if she called again to tell her to call me at this number. I closed our conversation by saying, "Buddy, something strange is going on and I don't know which way to turn. Maybe tomorrow by the time I see you, I will have a better direction."

Robert, Janet and I discussed the case, and we all felt that Kali knew more about what was happening than she let on. We needed some kind of set-up to expose her. As we were kicking ideas around, Terry showed up.

Janet was a gracious hostess and made a pot of coffee that she served with some cake she had made the night before. I brought Terry up to speed on the case and told him about my need for a helicopter. He said he had a good friend who was captain of the Air Patrol and that he would make a call to him in the morning.

He wasn't sure if he could pull enough strings to get permission for a helicopter to be flown by a civilian on an out-of-state flight, but he was willing to try. I realized how bazaar all of this must sound, but I really needed to check out the Grand Canyon. Robert said he understood my feelings and agreed that I should give it a shot if Terry could get a helicopter.

We also agreed that I needed to get with Kali again in order to try to get some information from her. Since Scottie had the shop under control, I decided I would make another trip to ChemTec tomorrow.

During the night, I didn't sleep very well as a lot of "what-if's" kept rolling through my mind, not to mention being in a strange bed. It is hard for me to sleep well when I am away from home. I remembered back to the time when Dad took us boys camping, and I could sleep soundly on the hard-rocky ground, but those days are long past. I also remembered, with a smile, that Mom and Dad and others their age would say they couldn't sleep away from their own bed, and I thought that was ridiculous. Now I totally understood.

When it was daylight, I got up when I smelled the coffee brewing. Janet and I sat at the kitchen table talking as we drank our coffee, and she told me how happy she was to be in our family and that Robert was no doubt the love of her life. We talked about how hurt Robert had been when Linda was killed and how she felt uncomfortable trying to console him so soon after his wife's death, but she also had a pressing need to be there with him. She had lost her first husband and understood what Robert was going through. It all worked out beautifully and they had blended their two families together.

While we were talking, Richard and Rachel came through and ate a quick bowl of cereal before going out to catch the school bus. Soon Darrin, Janet's youngest, followed suit. I commented on how quickly they were growing up and how blessed Richard and Rachel were to have her in their lives as a mother figure. I asked about her older girls and where they were. She said Paige was in college at North Texas State University and Tiffany was working at Sears in Dallas and was engaged to be married next spring.

Our conversation was interrupted when Robert came dragging in rubbing the sleep from his eyes. I told him to get a cup of coffee as he looked like he needed it to wake up. Soon afterward, I headed to Ft. Worth.

I got to ChemTec a little before lunch and asked Kali if she could join me for a bite. She said she had brought her lunch, but I was welcome to join her. There was a small patio area just outside her office that had tables where employees could go. It was a relaxing place to have lunch. I went up the street and got a couple of hamburgers to go and rushed back for my lunch date.

I told her that I wanted to catch her up on what was happening. I told her about the strange telephone call about the Grand Canyon, but that I felt it was just a diversion and that I would soon be making arrangements to go to Yemen. I certainly had her attention as she asked why I felt the Grand Canyon was a diversion.

"It makes absolutely no sense for Ron and/or Tim to be held hostage in that canyon," I said. "What would be the point? All that's there is dirt, rocks, and a river. How could that possibly have any bearing on this case? It has to be a hoax in an attempt to mislead me. Besides, that is a huge canyon and someone could hide there and never be found."

Strangely, the more I talked, the more I was convincing myself that it was a hoax and that it didn't make any sense for me to try to go there. This would have absolutely nothing to do with the weapons of mass destruction that Yemen wanted.

"Sonny, it does seem strange. In fact, it's so strange that no one would think of using that as a diversion. I think there is something to it."

"Do you know of a link between the chemical research and the Grand Canyon?" I asked.

"None," she said.

I couldn't tell if she was telling the truth or not, but she certainly sounded convincing. The rest of our lunch conversation was a light, unrelated conversation. As I was getting ready to leave, surprisingly, she asked me if I had any dinner plans for the evening. I told her I had plans with my cousin and his family, but maybe another time we could get together. Even though I wanted to trust her, I had a gut feeling that she wasn't being honest with me and was perhaps trying to set me up.

I got back to East Texas mid-afternoon, and as soon as I walked in, Robert said, "Hey, Sonny. I'm glad you are back. I have some good news and some bad news. Terry stopped by and said he was not able to get a helicopter from the game warden department. There were too many liability issues plus departmental procedures. That's the bad news, but the good news is that he found out an old retired Texas Ranger buddy of his owns an aviation company in Hillsboro that has helicopters to rent.

Hillsboro Aviation rents choppers to news teams, Hollywood, and some offshore drilling companies. Terry called him and explained that he has a cousin who needs to do some investigative work that would require the use of a helicopter. His friend then told him that was not a problem. He said, as a friend, he would let you use one at no charge. You would only need to provide the fuel. He also added that his helicopters are insured in case something should happen to one of them. All you need to do is go by the Hillsboro Aviation place and sign a rental agreement with all charges waived. So, there you are – you have a helicopter at your disposal!"

I couldn't believe what I was hearing! This really made it necessary for me to make a decision as to what to do. Robert could almost read my thoughts when he said, "You don't have much to lose. It's not going to cost you much to take a look." He was right. It really wouldn't cost me much at all other than the fuel and some time to take this helicopter deal. Since I knew I couldn't rest until I gave it a try, I decided to do it.

It was late in the afternoon, but I called Hillsboro, and as luck would have it, there were still some people in the office. I told them who I was, and soon I was talking to Chris Stoker, Terry's friend and the owner of the shop. After talking for a few minutes, I told him that I'd be there at about ten o'clock in the morning.

After I finished that call, it was time for Robert to close his office, and we went back to his house. The kids were already home from school and were in the barn tending to the cows and horses. I was impressed that they were performing their tasks without complaining about it. Robert and Janet have a lovely family, and for some reason, when I thought of that, my thoughts returned to Kali.

After we finished eating supper and were sitting around the table, Scottie called and said I had received an anonymous call. He gave the caller Robert's number. Within a few minutes, the phone rang and someone with a muffled voice said, "Scroggins - no hoax. Get me - Grand Canyon." Since Robert is a P. I. (private investigator), he had a recorder on his telephone that recorded all calls. We played the recording over and over trying to pick up on something that might help us decide who it might be. It did confirm to me that Kali definitely had a role in this since the hoax idea was mentioned only to her. That was the seed I planted when I was only with Kali.

Near the end of the recorded message, there was some loud background noise that sounded like a low-flying jet airliner. "Perhaps the call was made from around DFW or Love Field Airport," I said.

Robert said, "Yeah, or LAX or the airport in Phoenix, or anywhere else in the world." After he said that, I knew he was right. That noise was really not much help for us as I had hoped it would be.

That night I fell asleep wondering if "Grand Canyon" was referring to a place or if it was some kind of code name.

The next morning, I was up and off early heading toward Hillsboro Aviation. Just as planned, I arrived a few minutes before ten and was met by Chris Stoker.

After a few minutes of conversation and a cup of coffee, we made our way out to the flight line where there were eight Robison R44 helicopters anchored down. We removed the tie-downs on the first one we came to, and after performing a visual walk-around inspection, both Chris and I climbed into the cockpit with me in the pilot's seat and behind the controls. Before letting me fly off in his helicopter, he wanted to be sure I knew something about flying, so I was to take him up for a test flight.

Once inside and seated, I told Chris that it had been a long time since I had been inside one of these, and this one was quite a bit smaller than the Cobras we flew in Vietnam. It took a few minutes for me to become familiar with where everything was. But once I did, it was like riding a bicycle – you never forget. Before taking off, I needed to get a feel for the aircraft. Much of flying a helicopter is based on feel and your instincts, so to help me get a mental baseline for the feel, I changed the pitch on the rotor blades with the cyclic stick. Then I moved the collective pitch control located on the left side of the pilot's seat to change the pitch angle on all the blades at the same time. Both of these controls seemed a little stiff to me, but they seemed to work just fine.

Finally, I pressed the anti-torque pedals located in the same position as the rudder pedals in an airplane, but without being in the air, it was difficult to tell how much they moved the nose of the aircraft.

After some ten or fifteen minutes of familiarization, I started the engine and soon the rotors were turning. I called the control tower and asked for permission to take off, which was given. Soon I pushed the collective position control, and up we went! What an exhilarating feeling that I had almost forgotten! Chris wanted me to hover about ten feet above the ground for a few minutes while he filled out a flight chart. I think he really wanted to see how efficiently I could control the aircraft before we went for a test ride.

Then we were off and flying over the countryside of central Texas. The day was clear, and we could see for miles in all directions. To the north, we could see the skyline of Dallas, but in the other directions, all we could see was an open range dotted with a few farmhouses and barns.

After about twenty minutes of flying, we returned to the airfield and landed. Chris commended me on how well I controlled the helicopter, especially on my hovering skills and landings. I told him those were two critical things we had to do in a rescue mission, and in years past, I had a lot of experience at both.

We went back to the office where I signed a rental agreement with all charges waived just as Terry said. Chris really didn't ask any questions about my mission, but he understood that it was some kind of secret rescue and said, "Sonny, keep the helicopter as long as you need it. I trust that you can handle it fine and will take care of it. Your biggest problem will be getting flight space in the Grand Canyon area. It is so congested these days that it's hard to get in and out without being near some other helicopter. Be safe."

I thanked him, called Robert with an update, and then filed a flight plan to Arizona.

CHAPTER 5

gathered a few things from the car that I might need, including several detailed maps of the Grand Canyon floor that I copied at the library a few days ago. Since the R44 helicopter could only fly about 350 miles without refueling, I arranged my flight to stop at Lubbock, Albuquerque, and then Flagstaff. From Flagstaff, I'd make my voyage into the canyon.

I left Hillsboro about mid-day and knew I couldn't reach my destination before dark, so I decided to spend the night at the Albuquerque International Airport. It was after dark when I landed the chopper and walked across the tarmac to the terminals. I grabbed a bite to eat at one of the restaurants in the airport and then settled down on one of the couches for some shut-eye. Even though there were a lot of people coming and going, I did manage to doze off and actually slept pretty well.

The next morning, I was up and about early. After fueling and visually inspecting the aircraft, I was soon in the air again. I was surprised that the helicopter seemed to handle much easier than when I used it on the trial flight. As I flew over what was becoming mountainous terrain, a lot of Vietnam memories flashed through my mind. I was so glad this was not a war rescue mission.

I was in Flagstaff by noon, and after eating a hamburger, I headed for the south rim of the Grand Canyon. I had no trouble getting permission from the Flagstaff control tower to fly into the canyon. Perhaps, this is not the time of year when a lot of tourists want to go into it. I used the radio and found out that the weather was going to be partly cloudy with a thirty percent chance of snow flurries. I was glad I had packed a coat and blanket, but I wasn't prepared for any severe weather.

Within an hour, I was flying smoothly over the south rim of the canyon, when all of a sudden, it was as if the earth literally dropped out from beneath me! The sight of the Grand Canyon was breathtaking and more amazing than I could ever have imagined!

While I was descending toward the canyon floor, I wondered, "Now what?" Now that I'm here, do I expect to see Ron waving a white flag? Or should I look for a flare being fired up into the air? Maybe I could spot him and Tim riding the rapids on the Colorado River! What should I do now? I decided I had been very foolish to even think I could rescue those guys even if they were being held hostage. I also realized once again that I had no idea who made those phone calls saying they were in the Grand Canyon. Oh well, now that I'm here, I should just try to enjoy myself and consider this to be a mini-vacation.

I made a circle around a seemingly level area where I thought I could land the chopper. I was able to set down without any problems. Since the area was sheltered from the late afternoon sun, it was getting dark and cold rather quickly.

Rather than flying back to Flagstaff, I decided to camp out in the canyon for the night. I had always enjoyed camping in east Texas when I was a boy. Hopefully, I would enjoy this too and would later remember it with fond memories. I scouted around for enough loose wood to build a campfire, and by the time it was blazing, I was so thankful I had built it as the cockpit thermometer read 28 degrees. Even though I was wrapped in the wool blanket I brought, I was shivering cold and again wondered why I was here and especially why I had made the decision to camp here overnight!

The next morning, when I woke up, I was very cold from the frigid air and very stiff from lying on the hard ground. It was almost daylight, and when the sun began to shine on the west wall of the canyon, I had never seen a more beautiful sight! I can't describe the different colors that nature provided with the assorted rock formations and types. The rising sun seemed like a slow descending curtain as it made its way from the top of the rim toward the valley floor. I was mesmerized by the whole experience and thought the trip was worthwhile regardless of the way it might turn out.

I didn't bring any camping provisions because of limited space on the helicopter, so all I had for breakfast were some day-old donuts and instant coffee. However, at that moment in time, it tasted as good as a gourmet meal.

I built another fire, and after standing by it and moving around some, my body began to thaw out and function to some degree. While I stood with a cup of coffee in my hand, admiring the sights and wondering what to do in my search effort, a couple of hikers walked up. They immediately started talking to me with most of the conversation being about the helicopter. They said it was not uncommon to see other hikers camping overnight, but seeing a helicopter was very rare. I think they must have thought I was a government agent or something by the way they seemed fidgety the whole time we were talking.

I told them I had an interest in searching inside of caves and hopefully one day I could write a book about them. I then asked if they had seen any when they were hiking that I can explore. They said there were a few up the river away, but none very close to where we were. I thanked them for the information before they wandered on.

Soon, I was once again up in the air flying as close to the rock canyon walls as I felt was safe, and I was searching for a cave that looked as if it had any type of traffic near the entrance. I saw numerous crevices that could easily be openings to a cave, and some had water dripping off them like small waterfalls. I saw a few that appeared to have a trail leading up to them, but I assumed they were animal trails and didn't bother to stop.

I realized I was getting low on fuel and knew I had to go back to Flagstaff to refuel the tank. As I made a turn to prepare to lift up out of the canyon, I saw a cave with a man and a woman in front of it. They watched and waved as I flew past. I wondered if they were campers or perhaps guards for the hostages.

After refueling, I returned and landed the helicopter near where I thought I had seen the couple. Even though the terrain was treacherous, I worked my way back to where I thought they were. I then realized that the cave opening was on a plateau some fifteen to twenty feet above where I was, and I could see no way to get up there. I walked around looking for a way up, but nothing appeared obvious. Just as I was about ready to give up, I noticed a crevice that looked as though I might be able to climb through it up to the plateau.

It was treacherous. As I climbed, I thought if I should fall and break a leg or something, no one would ever know where to look for me. I thought I could die down here and only the buzzards would know about it. I told myself I needed to stop having negative thoughts and to enjoy this magnificent view. I made it up to the plateau without incident. Once I was on the plateau, I easily found the entrance to the cave.

I cautiously made my way inside the cave and waited a few minutes for my eyes to adjust to the darkness. Then I eased deeper inside. After a short distance, I could hear voices, and the closer I got,

I could tell they were coming from a man and a woman. I supposed they were the ones I had seen earlier. I finally got close enough to see them, and I watched for a while as they frolicked around. Finally, I decided they were not part of a kidnapping ring, so I made some noise as I made my way to where they were.

I told them I was looking for a friend that I thought might be in one of these caves and asked if they had seen anyone else around. To further cover my tracks, I also told them that I was doing research on caves in order to write a book and that my friend was helping me do the research. I told them I had gotten lost from him and was looking into various caves in hopes he was in one of them. It troubled me that I was finding lying to come so easily. They told me they hadn't seen anyone, but they really weren't looking for others as they were on their honeymoon. I thought this was a pretty unique place to spend a honeymoon. I might want to try it myself someday. I excused myself and left without telling them my name.

As I was making my way back toward the crevice, I heard a rattling sound and immediately felt excruciating pain in the calf of my left leg just above my ankle. As I fell to the ground, I noticed a large rattlesnake slithering through the rocks. I was surprised to see a snake in this cold weather, but here he was. I yelled for help, but the couple in the cave apparently could not hear me. My only hope was to get back to them. I could tell with each breath that my strength was weakening. When I got to the cave entrance, I collapsed, and everything began to circle around and around.

The next thing I remembered was waking up to the warmth of a campfire inside the cave. I asked what happened. The honeymooning couple said they heard something in the front of the cave, and when they went to check, they found me lying on the ground mumbling "rattlesnake." The young man said he immediately began to look me over and found the puncture wounds on my leg. The girl said her husband was a pre-med student in Phoenix, and he reacted just like an old pro. She said he took his first-aid kit and lanced the area that was bitten, and with the suction bottle, he was able to extract much of the venom. She said he also had some antibiotic tablets that he gave me.

I asked how long I had been here, and they said one full day and night, and for most of the first day, I ran a high fever. Now my temperature was back to normal, and other than having a sore leg, I felt fine. They gave me some hot stew to eat for which I was very grateful.

After eating, I expressed to them my gratitude for saving my life and wanted somehow to repay them for their kindness. However, they said just seeing me alive was already enough thanks to them. I remembered the little girl and the near-drowning incident at Lake Eli and told them that I understood.

Then I left and finally made my way back to the helicopter. My leg was hurting, but I could tell there was no infection as there were no red streaks. It was near mid-day, but I didn't know what day of the week it was. Even though I don't pray nearly as often as I should, or that my Scroggins Family members do, I fell on my knees and couldn't stop the tears from flowing as I thanked God for sending me those people who just saved my life. I imagine they will enjoy telling everyone how they spent their honeymoon nursing a man with a snake bite!

Before taking off, I carefully inspected the helicopter as I figured there had been ample opportunity for some curious by-passers to mess something up. In spite of several sets of footprints around the chopper, everything seemed to be alright. Finally, I fired her up and was soon in the air again. I kept investigating the canyon walls the best I could from the air, but nothing ever showed me any clues.

As the end of the day neared, I flew up and out of the canyon and back to Flagstaff. I really had no desire to sleep in the bottom of the Grand Canyon on the cold hard ground again! Once was enough for me. Inside the terminal, I was able to get a shower and a hot meal.

After I cleaned up, I called Robert and told him that I had had no luck at all and was about ready to head back home. He suggested that I give it one more day before coming home and said when I got there, he had some interesting information to share with me.

Now I was curious as to what he had discovered and could hardly wait to get home. The next morning, I was out early and resumed flying the canyon walls looking for anything that might lead me to the whereabouts of Ron and Tim. Part of the time, I was flying near the Colorado River which was majestic in and of itself with the white-water rapids and waterfalls.

Toward the end of the day, I had found nothing, which at this point, was really no surprise. I did see several tourist helicopters flying around as well as some groups riding mules down into the canyon and some riding back out. But there was nothing that would lead me to my rescue mission. I searched until I was low on fuel and needed to go back to Flagstaff.

The next morning, I headed back to Texas. I had flown most of the canyon walls and didn't know what else to do. By late afternoon, I drove up to Robert and Janet's house. Naturally, they wanted to know if I found anything and seemed to be disappointed to learn that I hadn't.

Likewise, I wanted to know what news they had for me. Robert said that when he and Janet went inside ChemTec, they had a concealed microphone that recorded all the conversations on a recorder inside their car. He said they had taken the recorded muffled message we received a few days ago on his telephone to a voice-analyzing expert in Dallas who was able to filter out the muffle and reconstruct the tape. From that reconstructed tape, he was able to do a voice comparison to the taped conversations that he had made.

"Guess what?" Robert said. "The phone call was from none other than Kali Huff!"

"Are you sure?" I asked, hoping that they all had it wrong.

"No doubt about it. I'm sorry to tell you that, Buddy, but the electronic analyzer compared the signal levels and there was clearly a match."

Well, this was somewhat of a surprise, but not totally. I had suspected for a while that she was involved but kept hoping I was wrong. "What next?" I asked.

"I don't know," Robert said. "That's your call, but I'd be very careful about what I tell her."

That night, I didn't sleep much, even though I was tired, because of everything that had happened. I needed to have a serious talk with Kali and try to get to the bottom of this although such a conversation with her might be life-threatening to me.

The next morning. I made the decision to go have a talk with Kali, but before I left, I called Scottie to check-in. I asked him to check on Fuzzy and make sure she has plenty of cat food. He told me things had really been pretty slow in the store and that the classes for the power company scuba divers were going fine. He said the students should be ready to get into the water next week. I told him I hoped to be home before then and would fill him in on everything when I got there.

As before, I got to ChemTec a little before noon. I asked for Kali, and she soon came and met me in the lobby. I told her that we needed to talk as I had some information to share with her. She agreed to go with me during lunch to a small city park not far from the company.

The park was nice with several picnic tables scattered beneath some large trees, and to my amazement, we were the only people there. We went to a table to eat some burgers that I had picked up, and as we were eating, I told her about my Grand Canyon venture, including my snake bite. She seemed very concerned about what might have happened from that bite. Finally, I said to her point-blank, "Kali, I'm very fond of you, and I want you to be honest with me. How are you involved in this case?"

"Well, I know what you know," she said. "I know that Tim and Ron are missing and that you are trying to find them. That's about it. Why do you ask?"

"No. You know more than that. I really need someone I can trust, and I had hoped that might be you, but I'm not sure now," I said.

"I don't understand," she replied in an innocent-sounding voice.

"Kali! Stop playing games with me! I want the truth. I know that you made the phone calls to me about the Grand Canyon, and for the life of me, I can't figure out why, but I will. However, it would be much easier if you would just level with me-- please!"

She looked like a kid that had just gotten caught with her hand in the cookie jar! Finally, she said, "Alright, you want the truth? I really don't know where Ron and Tim are, but both of them are my dear friends. I think they are in a confined laboratory in Yemen. Somehow, my long-lost brother got in with the political leaders of Yemen, and I don't know how or why I got involved.

I have received threatening messages saying that unless I diverted any investigation away from Yemen, my brother would personally execute Ron and Tim. I don't know how he knew we were friends. In fact, I don't know how he even knew I worked for ChemTec. All of that is scary. Regardless, I didn't make the first call to you, but I did make the one to lead you down the wrong path. Somehow, I feel they know about you and that you are trying to rescue Ron and Tim."

"Kali, can I trust you, and will you help me?"

She answered yes to both questions. I told her that I'd get back to her in a few days. But for now, I really needed to go back home. Before I left, she gave me her home telephone number but cautioned me about the possibility of her phone being bugged. She said she didn't know for sure, but she suspected that it was.

I left and went back by Robert's before heading home. I told him what Kali had said and that I felt she was telling the truth. He cautioned me again about not giving her too much information. Then we went back to the original message that said, "Can't talk. With friend. Grand Canyon."

"What do you think it means?" Robert asked.

I said I had assumed it was from Ron and the "with friend" meant he was with Tim, but the Grand Canyon part is what baffled me. Perhaps, it is some kind of code. Then Janet said the most obvious thing that I was overlooking. She asked, "Does Yemen have a Grand Canyon?"

I didn't know. I had assumed the message was speaking of the Grand Canyon in the United States, but I know that parts of Yemen are very rugged, and it could certainly have a "Grand Canyon." Now I wanted to go to the library and research Yemen before going home. The library would close in a couple of hours, so I should still be able to get home before dark.

When I started reading about the country of Yemen, I was amazed at what I discovered.

CHAPTER 6

As I studied the geography of Yemen, I was amazed at the mountain ranges along the coastline of the Red Sea, Gulf of Aden, and the Arabian Sea. My research informed me that the mountains were jagged peaks that jutted from an elevation of a few hundred feet on the coastal plains to well over 12,000 feet. Although the terrain was flat near the sea, it appeared that it quickly escalated into a very rugged mountainous range with peaks equivalent to our Rocky Mountains.

I also learned that the mountains were separated into Western and Central Highlands. The Western Highlands were along the Red Sea and had very high peaks that had relatively fertile soil with sufficient and plentiful rainfall.

The Central Highlands were more like a plateau of about 6,000–10,000 feet with rolling hills, small knolls, and a few prominent peaks. But what really caught my attention was that the highland regions had what were called "river valleys." I assumed this was what we would call canyons.

As I read more in one of the encyclopedias, I saw that one of the largest canyons, or river valley, was sometimes called "The Grand

Canyon." There wasn't a lot of information about it other than an aerial picture that showed a river in the canyon basin similar to our Grand Canyon. Perhaps, this is the place the anonymous message that I received meant! I had the gut feeling that somewhere along that river in the canyon, Ron and Tim were being held as hostages.

If Ron had suspected this was where Tim was being held, it would explain why he needed a helicopter and a scuba diver. A chopper could get close, and a diver could penetrate the facility. I felt that I was really onto something now!

It was closing time, and I was the last one to leave the library. Before heading back to Norton, I swung by Robert's to share with him what I thought I had discovered. Both he and Janet felt that my hunch might be right.

All the way to Norton, I was thinking about ways of pulling off this unusual mission. Where were they exactly? How would I get a helicopter? How much scuba equipment would be needed? If I located the facility, how could I find Ron and Tim? There were so many unanswered questions that I didn't even know where to start. With all of this running through my mind, the drive on the way to Norton seemed to fly by.

It was good to get home and to see Fuzzy. She was always glad to see me. After I got settled, I called Scottie and told him that I was home and would be in the shop tomorrow morning. That night I slept better than I had in a long time.

As was my custom, I got to the shop at least thirty minutes before opening time, and also, as usual, Scottie was already there and had the coffee made. We sat in the office where I gave him a quick update on what had happened. He was amazed at what I told him, especially about the rattlesnake bite and how the Lord must have been looking after me. He didn't know any more about Yemen than I did. In fact, he had never heard of Yemen before last week when he was trying to help me come up with some rescue ideas. We both agreed that a key player had to be Kali. Perhaps, she knew some contacts from the country of Omen that might be able to help. After all, it was their country for which chemical warfare was being developed. Surely, they would have some interest in the rescue of the lead scientist on the project.

It was time to open the shop, but there were no customers when we unlocked the door, so Scottie and I kept talking and catching one another up on things. He reminded me that the first scuba swimming class was tomorrow night and that I needed to get all the equipment ready for the six divers. That would take a good part of the day as each tank needed to be filled with air.

By late afternoon, I had everything ready to go and prepared an invoice for the *SET Power Company* to buy the equipment for each student. It's important for each diver to have his own equipment and to be familiar with how it operates.

That night, I called Kali and remembering what she said about the possibility of her phone being bugged, I kept the conversation casual and social. We talked about getting together next weekend. I suggested that she come down to Norton for a day as I'd love to show her around the town. She said that sounded like fun, but she didn't think she could come then as she had volunteered to help with a fundraiser for cancer research Saturday morning.

I then suggested that I come pick her up and that the two of us drive down to east Texas for the afternoon. She liked that idea, so I set the time to get her for 1:00 P.M.

The next afternoon, I loaded all of the scuba equipment into the back of my suburban and headed for Beaumont to teach the scuba class. Again, I kept thinking about the Grand Canyon in Yemen, and again I had more questions than answers. One thing in my favor was that I already had an out-of-country passport. I got it several years ago when I was often going to Central America to go diving.

I arrived at the site before the students did and had the gear unloaded beside the pool. As they arrived, they were glad to see me as I had missed the previous several classes. We spent the first hour going over the gear so they would be familiar with each item. I emphasized that the most crucial part was the breathing apparatus which included the regulator, hoses, mouthpiece, mask, and gauges. Since the company was paying for the equipment, I bought them the more expensive digital gauges instead of the analog gauges.

Finally, we were in the water. I had them go out into four feet of water where they had to bend over and put their head underwater and breathe through their equipment. After they became comfortable with breathing underwater, I had them lie on the bottom of the pool for about twenty minutes. By doing this, they became more comfortable with their equipment as well as prolonged breathing underwater. The water was only four feet deep, so they could stand up if necessary.

After the session, we discussed what we had done, and I found out that two of the six students were smokers, which meant their breathing was more rapid than the non-smokers. I reminded them of how crucial it was to monitor their gauges because the smokers would use up their air supply faster than the non-smokers. If a smoker and non-smoker were paired up as buddies, it might lead to a problem. To prove my point, I had each student report on how much air he had used, and the smokers had used about 30 percent more oxygen than the non-smokers, which meant they took three times as many breaths.

When class was over, I decided to head back to Norton instead of staying the night in Beaumont. As before, I drove with my thoughts on Yemen. I needed an aerial photograph of that area, but I had no idea how I could get it unless Kali had some contacts over there who could get one for me. I was very eager to talk with her.

The next morning, I called Kali and told her I had missed her and would like to see her before the weekend. I made the conversation sound romantic in case we were being monitored. We agreed on an evening date. I left work a little early and picked her up at 7:00. We went to a nearby restaurant and asked for an isolated booth. It was good to see her again, and for a few minutes, our conversation was casual. I then told her that I needed a contact in Omen who could provide me information on how to get into Yemen and what I should expect. She said she didn't know of such a person, but I pushed the point a little harder.

"Surely, you have some names of people who came to your company as customers to discuss this project, and there must be someone who comes and inspects the progress. There have to be some names in the files," I said.

Finally, she admitted there probably were some names of visitors, but she would be violating their security if she revealed them. I appreciated her loyalty to security, but at the same time, I was a bit taken aback that she didn't seem willing to help me. Then I suggested that she contact some of the people and see if she could set up a meeting between them and me. I told her to inform them of my mission and that I needed some cooperation from them. Ron had been missing for about six weeks, and I was no closer to finding him than in the beginning.

Kali said she would try but made no promises. I urged her to try really hard because if she couldn't help me, I didn't know where to turn. After our meal and conversation, I re-affirmed our weekend date to East Texas, and then I drove back to Norton.

The next few days were rather slow and uneventful. This gave me time to go to the library and study some more about Yemen. The more I studied, the more intrigued I became. The mountainous terrain I was researching seemed very likely to me to be the mountains where Moses received the Ten Commandments. I couldn't be sure, but it was somewhere in that neighborhood. Perhaps, I could disguise myself as an archaeologist searching for Biblical artifacts. But if I did that, I would probably have to get some type of government permit, which was unlikely to be given, especially on short notice.

Soon, I was back in the pool with the scuba class for swimming session number two. This time they had to go down in the deep end of the pool which was about ten feet deep. One of the things I had them do was to let some water fill their mask and then clear it of the water. We did that a few times, and then I had them pull their mask off and put it back on. Sometimes, when diving, the shock of the cold water hitting one's face causes a panic sensation, so they needed to be prepared if they ever experienced that feeling.

While going through this exercise, one of the smokers had a coughing attack, and he immediately panicked and pulled his mask off, removed his mouthpiece, and headed for the surface. I grabbed him, pulled him back down, forced the mouthpiece back into his mouth, and calmed him down enough to get his mask back on him.

During the discussion after the swimming session, we talked about panicking and I re-emphasized that if it should occur to them, they must keep their mask on and not try to rush to the surface. "If you need to cough or sneeze, you can do that with the mask on with no problem. But whenever you rush to the surface, there is the risk of getting "bends" which is a painful experience." One of the guys asked me what the "bends" were. I told him the main cause of it is a change in pressure and what it does to the nitrogen in our body. It causes pain and causes the diver to "bend over" — thus the name.

As we dismissed the class, I told them next week we would meet at the power plant lake and do some lake diving. We would do that during the day, so they would need to plan with their supervisors to be off work for that session.

The next day, Scottie and I had a pretty good rush of customers during lunch. But finally, things had eased a little when a man came in and was talking with Scottie. I was in my office and noticed

Scottie pointing in my direction and then saw the man coming my way. I got up and walked to the door to greet him.

"Hello," he said. "Are you Mr. Scroggins?"

I told him that I was, and he said, "I'm Armand, and we need to talk."

"Yes, sir," I said, "Please come in." I motioned him into the office and pushed the door closed. There was no one else in the shop other than Scottie, so I felt that we should be free to talk.

By his appearance and his name, I suspected Armand was from Omen, and I was right. He said he had been contacted by Kali and was told of my involvement in trying to rescue a couple of missing researchers in which he had a keen interest. I noticed that he was careful with his choice of words so as not to compromise the program's identity, although I already knew about it. He said that his government was agreeable to assist me in my efforts up to a point so long as they were transparent. I told him that I understood, and he then asked what I needed.

I told him I had several needs. One was a good aerial and topographical map of the region in Yemen known as the Grand Canyon. I also needed some type of transportation from here to there, and once I got there, I would need a helicopter. He said he would see what he could arrange.

"Anything else?" Armand asked.

"As a matter of fact, there is. I will need some way to get out of the country once the rescue is made. That will require some coordination with someone else. I can't pull it off by myself."

"I understand," he said. "Let me see what I can work out, and I'll be back in touch." Then he left the shop. Immediately Scottie rushed in and wanted to know the details as he had also suspected who the strange visitor was. I shared with him what he said, and for the first time, it seemed that there might be a way for me to make the rescues.

Saturday I was running a little behind and picked Kali up at her apartment about 1:30 P.M., and we headed for East Texas. She had never been to that part of the state before and was looking forward to the trip as well as meeting some of my family. I was looking forward to being with her and I wanted to show her off. As we were driving out of Dallas, I told her about my visit with Armand and thanked her for making the arrangements for that contact.

She told me she already knew about the meeting, and that she received a package late yesterday that had a detailed map along with a note attached that said, "For Scroggins." As she was talking, she was digging in her purse for the package. I was impressed with how fast that had happened. This whole operation is certainly not being run by amateurs!

We continued to discuss the mission and wondered if it might help to disguise our intent by going there together pretending to be a couple. She wasn't sure she could be away from work longer than a week, plus I wasn't too keen on getting her that close to the danger zone, although the idea of spending that much time with her had its appeal. I also had to admit I liked the idea of us being a couple.

The time passed quickly, and we soon drove up to Robert and Janet's house. They were both outside and came over to meet us before we got out of the car. Kali immediately recognized them as being the "auditors" who came into *ChemTec*, and she turned to me and said with her cute smile, "Why you rascal!" I smiled back with no comment.

We all went into the house for some cake that Janet had just taken out of the oven along with some coffee and/or hot chocolate. It didn't take long for Kali to feel comfortable and welcome. The kids were spending the night at Ben and Mary Ann's, so their bedroom was free for Kali should we want to spend the night. Kali thanked them for the invitation but declined as she had no provisions for staying overnight. I wished she had as I'd love for her to go to church with us Sunday morning, but maybe another time.

After a nice visit with Robert and Janet, I drove her around town and out to the orphanage where I introduced her to Ben and Mary Ann. While we were there, Little Pete and Jean stopped by and I introduced Kali to them and told her that they were Robert's parents. I could tell that she wasn't used to this many family members being around one another as her family was small and had a strained relationship.

On the way back to Ft. Worth, all Kali could talk about was my family and how much she had enjoyed the afternoon. I told her this didn't have to be the last time, and she said, "I hope not."

After I dropped Kali off at her apartment, I decided to go back to Norton instead of East Texas. This time, instead of thinking so much about Yemen, my thoughts were on Kali and how much I enjoyed being around her, and how she seemed to blend right in with the Scroggins Family. I wondered if she might be the right one for me. It was a little past midnight when I got home, and I was dog tired, so I went straight to bed without checking my mail or my telephone messages. I figured I could look at all of that in the morning.

I slept until about 8:30 the next morning, which was really late for me as I was normally up two hours or so earlier than that. I didn't have any mail and only one phone message about scuba diving classes. I decided not to go to Bible Class but only to the worship service as I wanted to start looking over the information that Kali had given me.

The aerial photos were most impressive. The detail was phenomenal. As I placed them in order on the kitchen table, I noticed some type of facility on the river's edge several miles inland from the sea. I wondered if that was where the hostages were held. The pictures were numbered, and I called Kali and asked if she could get me a closer view of photo 5C.

Then I studied the topographical map around that region. It was very rugged with what appeared to be steep cliffs and deep ravines. Before I knew it, it was time to leave for church, so I put the maps back inside the envelope and took them with me for safekeeping.

When I got back home after services, I sensed that someone had been inside my house. Although nothing was broken or messed up, it seemed to me that the newspaper had been moved and books on the floor were in a different order. While I couldn't say for sure, several things were different from what I thought I remembered. If my hunch was right, for what were they looking? Nothing seemed to be missing, so I ruled out burglary.

All of a sudden, the thought occurred to me that maybe they were looking for the maps! If so, then why? There is nothing classified about maps. More importantly, if they were looking for the maps, how did they know I had them? Now the aura of suspicion was cast back on Kali! Why did I feel so comfortable with her and feel that I could trust her on the one hand? However, I'm still having doubts that she might be 'setting me up.' Finally, I dismissed it as just my imagination and that I was being paranoid.

Later that afternoon, I received a telephone call from Armand saying, "This is Armand. Meet me tomorrow at 10:00 in the library for details." Then he hung up before I could get in a word.

Needless to say, the rest of my afternoon was filled with apprehension and questions. Why was Armand's conversation so short? Was he fearful of a phone tap? Would he or I be an open target tomorrow? What would have happened if I had not been home to answer the phone? What library? Did he mean the library here in Norton? I guess that is where I will go and hope it is the right one.

The next morning, with little sleep the night before, I made my way to the shop and told Scottie what had happened. He was also baffled and cautioned me to be on the alert. I assured him that I already was. Then about 9:30, I asked him to "man the shop" as I was headed for the library. As I was walking out, his final remark was, "Good luck."

CHAPTER 7

I was at the library a few minutes early and took a seat at a table near the window. I hoped this was the library Armand meant. I was watching out the window for him to drive up, but I never saw him. Finally, it was the time he had told me to meet him, and he was nowhere to be seen. I was beginning to wonder if I had misunderstood or had been stood up or was at the wrong library. As I was starring outside watching for him, he walked up behind me and said in his foreign accent, "Good morning, Mr. Scroggins. May I join you?"

Being startled, I quickly turned around and replied, "Of course! Please have a seat." We exchanged a few courteous comments before he got to the purpose of the meeting. I wondered how in the world he had gotten in here without me seeing him!

He told me that he had made some cooperative arrangements with his people, but he was not at liberty to divulge it all to me at this time. What he did say was that I was to leave tomorrow morning to fly to Gibraltar, Spain. Again, I couldn't believe that things were happening so fast! He said when I got to Gibraltar, I was to go to slip 41 at the wharf and board a cargo ship that was headed to Aden, Yemen. My contact person on the ship would be a man named Jared. He is the ship's captain. Armand said that I would be taken on board as a newly hired hand and that no one else would know of my mission.

He said that once we got near Aden, Jared would give me instructions on where to go and who to meet. As he finished telling me details of the arrangements, he slipped me airline tickets from Shreveport to Atlanta, Georgia, and from there I would fly transatlantic to Spain. He also gave me an envelope that he said contained $500 in Spanish currency. Then he asked if I had any questions.

I had a million questions! But I asked what I was to do should something go wrong or if the plan got interrupted. He simply smiled and said, "Improvise." By that, I understood that I was all alone in this mission and there was no backup to call on. This really made me feel uneasy, but what else was I to do?

I wondered why I felt such an urgency to try to rescue those two men! One I had never met and the other one I hadn't seen in years until the brief encounter recently. It was really no concern of mine in the first place. But somehow, I knew that I must continue with my quest. I realized that I may never be able to return home and that I may never see any of my beloved family members again.

Then I asked if I should take scuba gear, winter clothing, etc. He again smiled and said, "Go casual and travel light. You will be provided all that you need."

Then Armand got up, shook my hand, and said, "The success of this mission is to remain anonymous. The less people know, the better your odds. Good luck, Mr. Scroggins," and then he turned and walked out of the library. I continued to sit there stunned and scared. At least, when I was in Vietnam, I had comrades around me for support. Plus, I was in better physical condition then than now, although I was still in pretty good shape because of all my diving.

Should I tell Kali or Mom and Dad or any of my family? Or should I just vanish for who-knows-how-long? Once I leave, will my place be ransacked to make it look like I was kidnapped which is possibly what happened with Ron? I was really beginning to feel uneasy. I knew nothing about Armand other than he allegedly was sent because of Kali's request, and for that matter, could I trust her?

I paused for silent prayer and fervently prayed for safety, guidance, and wisdom. Finally, I got up and feeling weak in the knees, I made my way to the suburban and back to the shop.

I guess I didn't do a very good job of concealing my feelings because when I walked in, Scottie immediately asked what was wrong. We didn't have any customers, so we went into the office where I told him all that happened. I really felt relieved that someone else knew of my plans in case I never showed up again. We discussed what would be the best way to handle the secrecy of the mission. Finally, both agreed that in about ten days, he would call Robert and Janet and fill them in on the details and ask them to tell Mom and Dad. About a week later, he would call Kali.

We both felt that Kali already knew what was happening, and we both wondered if I was walking straight into a trap and would be held hostage in Yemen for the rest of my life. I shivered at the thought and asked myself for the hundredth time WHY I would even consider doing such a foolish thing. It was not as if I was trying to rescue anyone in my family or even close friends. I couldn't explain even to myself why I trusted Armand and why I would willingly leave our country in search of Ron and Tim. Why did I feel like they were somewhere in that Grand Canyon simply because I received a phone call that merely said, "Grand Canyon"?

I spent the rest of the day making travel plans. I asked the post office to hold my mail; I alerted the utility company that I would be using only the minimum services for a while, and I had the newspaper and trash pick-up stopped until further notice. I didn't worry about the shop as I trusted Scottie to manage the business, and he would either have to put the scuba classes on hold until I got back or finish the certification process himself. I was okay with whatever he decided to do about that.

Since the power company paid us for the training, it would be our responsibility to ensure that they had an instructor. Scottie said he would take care of that and for me not to worry about it. I also told him if he needed to hire some help, feel free to do so as I had no idea when, if ever, I'd be back. We both had tear-filled eyes as I walked out of the shop without either of us saying a word.

I packed a few things in a small carry-on bag and asked my neighbor to drive me to the bus station. I told him that I'd be out of town for a few days and asked if he would look after Fuzzy for me, and he was glad to oblige. I rode the Greyhound Bus to Shreveport and took a cab to the airport. I got to the airport a few hours before my flight was scheduled to depart, so I tried to get a little shut-eye in the lobby.

Soon, I was in the air headed for Atlanta and looking down from 35,000 feet was quite different from 10,000 feet in a helicopter. All the way, I had a gnawing in my stomach because of the uncertainty. I decided that part of the apprehension I was feeling was because I was not in control of any part of this mission. In all of the past circumstances I had encountered, I always felt that I had some control of what was about to happen, but not this time. I felt like a sitting duck with no idea from which way the shooting was going to come.

I had a two-hour layover in Atlanta before we were airborne to Spain. I sat next to a perfume dealer who tried to make conversation, but I was almost rude to him as I really didn't feel like talking nor did I trust anyone. I could sense that my personality was being altered and that I wasn't really myself. I wasn't sure I liked who I was becoming.

I finally dozed off and slept for several hours. The constant roar of the engines seemed to serve as a relaxer. While sleeping, I dreamed that Kali and I had gotten married and were in that Grand Canyon cave on our honeymoon. I envisioned how beautiful she looked in the glow of the campfire with the different colored rocks of the cave wall serving as a natural backdrop that enhanced her beauty. The stillness of the night was filled with romance as the silence was only interrupted by the sound of the crackling campfire.

I was awakened by the announcement to buckle up and prepare for landing. As we descended, I kept looking out the window trying to get some perspective on the layout and where the ship wharf might be in relation to the airport. I soon figured out that I was on the wrong side of the airplane to see any of that. Soon, we were on the ground and preparing to depart the plane, and I had that queasy feeling in my stomach all over again. When I stepped out the door onto the stairs that had been rolled up to the aircraft, I got my first view of "The Rock" as the Rock of Gibraltar was called. It was a marvelous sight as it jetted high into the air with a clear blue sky accenting its majestic beauty. I had often heard of this famous rock, but I never imagined I would actually see it. I thought, "There is the gateway to the Mediterranean Sea."

Once I entered the terminal, I had to make my way through customs. Fortunately, my passport was in order, and I was welcomed as a tourist. One obstacle was behind me, but I had to find the seaport and the ship wharves. Right away, I realized that I had a language problem. Why hadn't I thought about that earlier? I wondered if it was too late to get back on a plane and head back home, but I didn't have a ticket or the money to buy one. I tried to use sign language but had difficulty trying to describe a ship with my hands.

Finally, I went to the gift shop and looked at a city map. At least that gave me a perspective of where the airport was in respect to the seacoast. The airport looked to be only about three miles or so from the sea, but there were ports and docks from one end of the city to the other. Of course, the maps were not printed in English, but I bought one anyway and then found a taxi. I showed the taxi driver on the map where I wanted to go and wrote the number 41. He seemed to understand. At least, he was taking me somewhere.

About ten minutes later, we were at what was called the South Mole. It looked as though it could be the right place, so I pulled out some money, and not knowing the value of the money, I held it out for the taxi driver to select. He took some, nodded in gratitude, and then left. I really had no idea how much he took, but at least I was at the water.

I was standing at the entrance of what looked to be a long pier that went several hundred yards out into the water and then turned and paralleled the coastline. When it made the coastline turn, there was one ship after another lined up alongside the pier. Now I had to find wharf slip 41. Fortunately, Spanish and English numbers looked the same, and most of the slips were numbered. The Mole was wide enough for a hard surface road plus room for pedestrians. In addition, there were all kinds of shops and pubs lining the edges. I prayed and thanked God for a safe trip thus far and asked for His guidance and wisdom as I continued with my quest.

As I made my way down the strip, the first slip I came to was number 18. As I looked down the port, it seemed like there were ships docked for miles and miles. The only thing I knew to do was to start walking. The walking area was filled with quite a few people. I guessed them to be merchant sailors. After what seemed to be about a mile, I was in front of slip 26. At least I was making progress. I didn't know what time it was, but by the sun, I'd guess it to be about noon. With a little luck, I should be at the ship well before dark.

As I passed slip 32, I felt like I was being followed. All along the seaport, there were souvenir shops and small pubs. I stopped in one of the shops, and when I did, the two fellows I thought were following me also stopped a few feet behind. Now, what was I to do? Did they know me, and if so, were they friend or foe? After a few minutes of working up my courage, I made my way back to the walking area and headed on toward the ship. As I neared the two perpetrators who seemed to be waiting for me, I stopped in from of them and asked, "Who are you? Why are you following me and what do you want?"

I didn't know if they understood me or not, but after I asked them that question, one of them lunged at me while the other grabbed my bag and fled. I shoved the other one aside and started out after my bag. Fortunately, I was in good enough condition to have good wind, so I was able to outlast the thief in the foot race and eventually overtook him. When I did, I landed two solid blows to his jaw and grabbed my bag back. He didn't try to get up as he was too exhausted, and I never saw the second man again. I finally decided they were two hoods trying to steal from an American.

I had run so far that I was almost to slip 41, and the ship that was docked there looked ancient and dilapidated. Surely, this wasn't the ship I was supposed to board! I stood and watched for a while, and to my surprise, I saw a few men mingling around on its deck. Eventually, I made my way on board and asked for Jared. The sailors understood what I said, and one of them led me to what I presumed to be the captain's quarters. There was a stern-looking man with graying hair seated at a desk. I'd guess him to be in his mid-sixties.

"Are you Jared?" I asked.

"Yes, I am," he said to my surprise in English. "And who might you be?"

"My name is Scroggins — Sonny Scroggins. I was in hopes you were expecting me."

"No, Mr. Scroggins. What business do you have with me?" Jared questioned.

I was stunned that he wasn't expecting me! What was I to do now? Then instinctively, I remembered, "improvise." I said, "I was hoping I could apply as one of your crew hands. I'm new to these parts and need a job."

"Well, Mr. Scroggins, we can always use a good hand. Raviv will take you and show you to your quarters and then show you what you will be doing." I thanked him, and the man who had brought me to the captain's quarters now took me away and down below deck to a small room lined with bunk beds. He showed me one and implied that it was mine.

I thanked him and asked if he spoke English. He implied that he does, just a little. Still, I felt he knew enough for us to communicate. While I was putting my bag on my bunk, Raviv brought me several changes of clothes and said, "Change to these." Then he showed me where the shower room and latrine were located and indicated that I could change clothes in there.

As I was changing my clothes, I wondered if I was being set up and wondered why the captain hired me so quickly without asking me any questions. Is this the custom in Spain? Was Jared pretending not to recognize my name in order to see if I could be trusted? I changed quickly and all the while kept my bag nearby. I followed Armand's advice and really didn't have anything of any value in the bag except the Spanish currency, which I took out and put in my pocket. Once I was changed, I put my bag on my bunk and headed back up on deck.

When I arrived, Raviv met me and took me to some large cargo tanks where I joined six others in scrubbing the inside with some kind of solvent that smelled like Clorox. I had to wear a protective mask to keep it from burning my nose and eyes. I was thankful for my scuba training as the mask didn't bother me a bit, which seemed to surprise Raviv.

The tanks were huge, and I could tell that it would take several hours, if not days, to thoroughly clean one. We worked non-stop until near dark which was around five-thirty. Soon after quitting, we made our way to the chow hall for supper. By this time, I was exhausted and starving since it had been almost two days since I had any decent sleep or food. I don't know what we ate, but I ate a generous portion and enjoyed every bite.

All the crew seemed to accept me right away because they thought if Jared hired me, then I must be alright. Although most of them did not understand English, I could tell by their body language that I was welcome.

Right after supper, I took a shower and hit the bunk. I was really tired. The next morning, we were up early, had breakfast, and were back inside the tanks. About mid-morning, we took a break, and I had a chance to ask Raviv when we were scheduled to depart. He seemed to understand English better than he could speak it. He held up ten fingers, and I took that to mean in about ten days. That surprised me.

Somehow, I had thought they had been staying in port just to wait on me, and that when I arrived, we would set sail. I realized I wasn't as important to them as I had thought I was! Again, I was wondering if Jared was in on the plan or not. Once more, I felt out of control and didn't like it. Should I confront him or keep quiet? For now, I decided to let things ride to see what would happen. At least I didn't feel threatened. Before the day was over, most of the crew could say "Sonny."

The work was hard, but I was holding my own. I still had not talked to Jared since our first introduction, but I had seen him several times at a distance watching me. Finally, all the tanks were cleaned, and several large barges that were loaded with wheat and corn pulled alongside us and began filling our tanks with grain. I now figured our scrubbing was an attempt to clean the tanks in order to keep mold from attacking the grain.

While the tanks were being filled, most of the crew just stood around watching and we assisted where we could. While we were standing and watching, Raviv came up to me and I understood him enough to know that Jared wanted to see me in his office. Immediately my heart leaped into my throat. Was I in trouble, or was this the time we laid our cards out on the table? I didn't know, but I felt that within the next few minutes, I was going to find out. My heart was pounding as I headed up the ship stairs toward the captain's cabin.

CHAPTER 8

As I walked up to the captain's door, I noticed that it was closed. I knocked and rather quickly I heard an invitation to come in. When I entered, Jared asked me to sit down. Then he offered me a beer or soda or something else to drink, to which I politely declined. From his friendly gestures, I figured this was not a meeting to discuss my work.

"My friend, Armand, told me that you would be coming to join us, but he also told me to keep quiet as to why you are here," Jared said as he quickly got to the point. "As far as all the rest of the crew is concerned, you are just a new hired hand. And by the way, you are making a great hand."

I thanked him for his compliment but was eager to find out some more about my planned mission. He went on to say that Armand didn't tell him much about the overall plan. He had only told Jared what he needed to know, which was to take me on board the ship and deliver me to Aden, Yemen. There I was to meet a contact named "Nadir." More than that, Jared did not know.

I asked him where I was supposed to meet Nadir, and he said he didn't know for sure, but his guess was that Nadir would find me.

Then I asked Jared where he was from. I wanted to know a little bit about the man I was trusting with my life.

He smiled and said, "Everywhere. I was born in the rural country of Omen but took to the sea when I was sixteen and have been at sea basically ever since." I asked him if he was married or had a family to which he said no. He said the sea was his home and the crew was his family. We continued talking, with me telling a little bit about me and my home life. After about an hour, it was time for me to leave, and as I stood to go, Jared said, "I like the Mercure Hotel in Aden."

I thanked him and told him that I would check it out. Then I made my way back to the deck and joined the other workers. The dockworkers continued to fill the tanks with grain, and by late afternoon, they were all full. Raviv came by and helped me understand that we were to pick up some additional cargo tomorrow and then ship out the following day. I appreciated his friendship even though we couldn't speak each other's language.

That night, I had a hard time going to sleep. My mind kept thinking about home and wondering if my family knew yet where I was. I felt confident that Scottie was taking care of the shop, but I still lay there thinking about little things that I missed — like coffee every morning with Scottie, Fuzzy sitting on my lap, and the warm greeting from the people in East Texas. I guess in short, I was homesick.

Then I started thinking about Kali and that I really missed her. But all the while, she was a real mystery and I still didn't know if I could trust her. I wondered if she knew I was gone or if she thought I had just quit calling her. I wondered if she missed me and thought of me as I think of her. Finally, somewhere deep into the night, I fell asleep.

The next day, more barges came alongside the ship and loaded three large crates onto the back of our ship. That took most of the morning, but early in the afternoon, Jared called the crew together and said we were loaded and that we had a couple of hours to go ashore for any last-minute items as we would be pulling out of the dock at 5:00 P.M.

I had no reason to go ashore, so I stayed behind in my bunk. Raviv stopped by, and in his broken English, he asked how I was doing. I used sign language to ask him how long we would be at sea. He replied as best he could, and I understood that it would be about ten or twelve days before we got to Alexandria, Egypt, and then another four or five days to Aden — depending on how backed up the Suez Canal was.

After a few hours, I heard the ship's foghorn sound two long blasts. I assumed that meant something was about to happen. Soon the crewmen were back on the ship, and I made my way to the deck to join them. After a bit, the ship tethers were loosened, and a tug slowly pulled us away from the dock. It wasn't long until the tug broke away, and we were moving slowly through the Gibraltar Harbor on our own power.

As we passed by the Rock of Gibraltar, I looked across the way and could see Morocco, Africa, in the distance. This was an interesting adventure for me as it was the first time I had ever seen any of this part of the world.

Slowly, we sailed through the Strait of Gibraltar into the Alboran Sea, and by dark, we were in open water with only the distant sparkle of lights flickering from the African coastline. When the sun went down, the night breeze became cool so all of us deckhands went below to our bunks. This was my first night to try to sleep with the sound of the engines running. Since our sleeping quarters were near the engine room, the noise was quite loud.

Before going to sleep, I watched the others play card games. One group was playing *Spades* while another was playing *Penny-ante Poker*. Meanwhile, a third group was playing something new to me. After a little while, I crawled under my covers and turned my back to the crew and attempted to tune out the noise for some sleep.

Actually, the sound of the ship engines, like the airplane engines, became rather soothing, and it didn't take long for me to fall asleep.

The next day, there wasn't a lot of work for us deckhands to do, so for the most part, we kicked back and enjoyed the ride. A few of them played shuffleboard, and I actually tried my hand at it but was not very good. I enjoyed myself more just looking at the beautiful blue water. It was quite different from the creeks in east Texas where I had grown up.

In the distance, I could see schools of fish splashing the surface, and I decided that one day I would like to return here to do some serious blue-water diving. By this time, there was no land in sight, but occasionally we could spot a small island. I wondered if any people lived on those islands, and if so, would they welcome an outsider like me to come visit and dive?

On the fifth day, Jared called for me to join him in his office, which I did. He just wanted to visit, and he showed me on the map where we were, which wasn't very far from Libya. He asked me if I was a Christian, and I affirmed that I was. Then he proceeded to tell me that near Libya was the Gulf of Sirte, also known as the Gulf of Sidra, which is where the Syrtis Sands are located.

He said those were the sands that the Apostle Paul and the ship's crew feared during the shipwreck episode we read about in the bible. Then he pointed to a dark spot on the horizon to our left and told me that was the island of Malta. I remembered reading in the bible that Paul spent a lot of time on the island of Malta. Perhaps I was in the very waters where Paul and some 275 others battled the treacherous forces of nature.

This was an awesome feeling. I thanked Jared for calling it to my attention. Then he told me that we should get to Alexandria tomorrow and unload the boxed crates and pick up three others, refuel and that the next day we would head for Yemen. Jared told me that if I wanted to go into town, he could exchange my Spanish pesos for Egyptian pounds.

Just as Jared had predicted, the next day, we were docked in Alexandria and were unloading the crated cargo. I didn't do very much. I connected the crane's hooks to the crates for lifting and unloading. We had the cargo unloaded before noon and by three, we had the new crates loaded and strapped down but had to remain in the dock for the rest of the day for fueling. So, I decided to go into town.

This was a typical port city. There were a lot of bars and exotic dance clubs. I went into one of the clubs, and the place was full of smoke and drunken merchant seamen. I felt very out of place and uncomfortable, so I didn't stay long. In fact, I didn't stay in town very long because it was dirty, crowded, and dreary to me. I was so glad that I didn't live in a place like this. However, I did drop a note to Scottie to let him know that I was alright and still alive.

After a few hours of looking around, I went back to the ship. When I walked into the bunk area, I saw someone dressed in a hooded jacket rummaging through my bag! While blocking the doorway, I asked him in a forceful voice what he was doing. Naturally, I startled him, and he tried to run past me and out the door, but my ole football days flashed back as I made a great open-field tackle. The man was much smaller than I, so overpowering him wasn't too difficult. Once the scuffling was over and he succumbed to me, I had him remove his hood so I could get a good look at him. When he did, I was shocked! It wasn't a fella at all, but it was a young girl! I asked her if she spoke English, but she didn't utter a word. I soon realized that I was getting nowhere with her, so I took her to Jared's office.

I told him what happened and told him that I wanted to know who she was and why she was looking through my things. Of course, he understood my concerns, considering my mission, so he began to talk to her in the Egyptian language. Soon, she was talking back, and all the while I was in the dark as to what they were saying. Finally, he turned to me and said that she was just a local girl who watched and saw that everyone left the ship and decided to try to find something of value to sell at the open market. Basically, she is a small-time thief. He said it was just by coincidence that she was looking into my things when I walked in. "Sonny, she is no threat to you."

I was relieved to hear that but was bothered that someone had gone through my things. Again, I was glad Armand had told me to travel casually and lightly. I could tell by the tone of his voice that Jared was giving this young girl the "once-over", and when he had finished, he motioned for her to get off his ship. Then we both smiled as we sat down in his cabin and enjoyed some strong, navy-quality, black coffee.

Jared said that tomorrow we should be in the Red Sea if we didn't have any problems getting through the Suez Canal. I asked what a problem could be, and he said, "Too many ships for one thing. If there are too many trying to get through at the same time, then it's like rush hour traffic in the city — very slow-moving. Then sometimes, some ships are being searched for some kind of illegal cargo. When that happens, everything comes to a halt until the investigation is completed. Hopefully, we will not have any of that tomorrow."

I was curious as to who might be doing the checking of the ships, so I asked him who the police agents for the canal were.

Jared said, "Initially, it was owned and controlled by Egypt until the big Suez crisis occurred back in the fifties. After that, the United Nations got involved and created the Suez Canal Association, *SCA* for short. Today, the SCA owns the Suez Canal and all areas, buildings, and equipment associated with it."

I was fascinated by what he was telling me. I had always heard about the Suez Canal but never gave any thought to its operation. "It sounds like the *SCA* is a pretty big outfit," I said.

"It sure is," Jared replied. "It's not uncommon for them to collect several million dollars a year in toll collections. For instance, tomorrow, I'll have to pay them a little over $5,000 U.S. equivalent dollars to pass through the Canal Zone."

I was stunned and asked why he had to pay such an exorbitant fee. He said it was simple. "You either pay the toll or spend four to six weeks sailing around the southern coast of Africa. Fuel cost alone would kill you not to mention your schedule delay. By comparison, we'll be in the Red Sea in about fifteen to twenty hours instead of weeks."

"Sounds like they are in a position to call all the shots," I said.

"They really are. They own both sides of the canal including all the businesses and the shipyard. They are the law enforcement agency along the canal and operate some fifty or more ships. In fact, they have a hospital on either end of the canal just for emergency cases. There is no doubt that they are the law of the canal and you do not want to get crossways with them."

I said I hoped we would not have any trouble tomorrow and decided it was time for me to turn in. I told Jared I had had enough excitement for one night. When I got back to my bunk, I kept thinking about the *SCA* and its impact on our world economy. I tried to imagine how hard it would be to control the traffic in a canal over 120 miles long with huge ocean liners fully loaded from all parts of the world going in both directions. Finally, I drifted off to sleep thinking about the Suez Canal.

Later that night, I was awakened by some of the crew coming in. They were pretty well looped, and it was obvious that they had been in the bars all night. Most of them staggered to their bunks and fell across them without even taking their shoes off. I was glad I was not in their shape and glad that I would not be feeling as bad as they will tomorrow.

After what seemed to be just a few minutes, we were all instructed by Jared over the intercom to man the deck. We were getting in position to enter the canal, and he wanted to make sure that we put forth a legitimate image with no cause for suspicion. We were to be friendly to the *SCA* patrol boats as they passed by, which was easy for me, but the rest of the crew really had to fake it as they were paying the price for their partying the night before.

Soon, to our surprise, one of the patrol boats came alongside us, and some men requested to come aboard. Jared welcomed them, but I was apprehensive about what might happen next.

CHAPTER 9

Six *SCA* officers made their way aboard our ship, and one who appeared to be the officer in charge went into the captain's office with Jared while the other five inspected the deck and cargo. We all remained together on deck and watched as the officers did their inspection. I wondered if they were looking for something in particular, or if they did this kind of inspection on every ship. If they did, I could certainly see why it takes so long to get through the Suez Canal Zone. I wished some of the crew members could speak English or that I could speak their language. Sign language is a hard way to communicate, and I had a lot of questions that I would like to have answered.

After a bit, the officer and Jared came out, and all the officers gathered in front of us. After giving us a good "look-over", the officer in charge singled me out and motioned for me to step forward. It was apparent I was different because of both my complexion and size. I was a good twelve inches taller than the rest of the crew and had lighter skin and hair. Immediately, I was apprehensive. Had Jared sold me down the river? Was I going to be arrested as a spy?

When I was in front of the officer, I stood at attention as he asked in perfect English, "May I please see your passport?"

I removed my passport from my wallet and handed it to him. He looked it over and said, "Mr. Scroggins, why are you on this ship, and where are you going?"

Now I wasn't sure what to say, because I didn't know what Jared had told him. Armand's word echoed ever so loudly, "Improvise!" I replied by saying, "I wanted to see different parts of the world, but I couldn't afford to pay for the trip. I decided to try to work my way as a cargo hand, and Captain Jared was kind enough to give me a job — so here I am."

He gave me a long glaring stare as if he doubted my story, but after a few seconds that seemed like several minutes, he returned my passport without saying another word. Then he and his men left the ship and headed somewhere else. I was really relieved, and my heartbeat started slowing back down to normal. I was seeing myself locked up in some Egyptian jail for who knows how long, or possibly forever.

Soon, our engines were engaged, and we began to inch forward. I assumed that meant we had passed the inspection and now it was just a matter of patiently maneuvering through the canal passage.

Once my nerves were settled, I really enjoyed the rest of the day. Both shorelines were dotted with some type of mariner businesses. There were ship repair places, radio shops, eating establishments, and there were also several scuba shops. For some reason, I was glad to see the scuba shops. My thoughts quickly went to my own shop, and I wondered about Scottie and the classes he was teaching and also about Fuzzy.

Later in the day, Jared called me to his office, and I was very eager to talk with him. When I got there, he asked about the brief interrogation I had received. I told him what the officer asked and what I said. He said that I did well. Being curious, I asked if the officer said anything to him about me, and he said he asked who I was and what I was doing on the ship. Jared said he told him that he picked me up in Spain as a crew hand and that I was a good worker. At least, our stories matched.

I asked Jared why he thought they singled me out. He said they mentioned something about a message I had mailed that got their attention. I had to think back about a message, and I told Jared that when I was on land yesterday, I mailed a note to my business partner to let him know that I was alright. All I said was, "Hey, Scottie, I'm at the Suez Canal on a cargo ship called The Libertine and all is well. Hope to see you soon."

"I don't know," Jared said, "But something about that message made them suspicious and they wanted to talk with you. I was worried that they might detain you here." He and I were both very glad they didn't. I couldn't imagine how anyone would have known I sent that note or what it said. I realized more than ever how much I needed to watch my back.

Then Jared got down some mariner maps and showed me where we would be going. He said it might be helpful to my mission if I was familiar with the surroundings. As he showed me the map of the Red Sea, one thing I noticed was that it was dotted with islands.

When I questioned him about it, he said we would, for the most part, be keeping those islands to our right because the water around them had many shallow spots and coral reefs. He said there is a deep channel where we will travel between the islands and the inland shores of Saudi Arabia and Yemen. He explained that when we approach Yemen, there will be a group of islands called the Farasan Islands. He added that those islands were rather desolate, and their biggest attraction was scuba diving and snorkeling.

As he was talking, he was showing me where they were on the map. As we looked at the map, I noticed many other smaller islands with no names. Jared said there were hundreds of small islands no larger than a few square miles, and because of their small size, they were mostly uninhabited. How in the world would I EVER find anyone who was hidden in places such as this? Again, I thought how foolish I was to even think about making a rescue. I regained my composure and asked him how deep the water was in the channel.

"It ranges between a thousand and sixteen-hundred feet deep," Jared answered.

"How close to land will we be?" was my follow-up question.

"We will be about twenty miles to the closest island, but when we go through the strait at the mouth of the sea, we will be about twenty miles from Africa and twenty-five to thirty miles from Yemen."

We continued to inch our way through the canal. After talking with Jared for several hours, I asked if it was alright if I went below deck for a nap. He had no problem with that because there was really nothing for us deckhands to do while we were at sea.

I guess I was more tired than I realized because I slept soundly until the next morning. When I got up, we had gotten through the Canal Zone and were out into the Red Sea. Jared said it would take about four days to get to Aden, Yemen, where we were to dock and unload part of our cargo. It was there that I was supposed to meet with Nadir. So far, things had progressed just fine, but I still felt out of control which bothered me a lot. I didn't like the "wait and see" game.

After I had a bite of breakfast, I stopped by to speak to Jared and to see if he knew anything more about my meeting with Nadir. He said he didn't, but once we were docked, someone would be contacting me with all the information I needed. I asked him if he knew Nadir, and he said he did and that Nadir was a stern, no-nonsense type of fellow that I didn't want to get crossways with.

Hearing that certainly didn't help my feelings any! I was beginning to regret ever getting involved in this whole mess. I really didn't need to be here. I should be back home tending to my scuba shop and courting Kali. I should be going to East Texas to eat some of Mary Ann's homemade apple pie. I should be stroking Fuzzy on the back. However, I had enjoyed my journey thus far and had seen many things I had never expected to be able to see.

My thoughts were interrupted by Jared asking me if I'd like to try my hand at the wheel. That sounded like fun and I jumped at the opportunity. I was familiar with some of the instruments, like the compass and pressure gauges, because they were similar to the instruments used in scuba gear. Jared instructed me on the charted course and what tolerance we had.

I quickly got the feel of the pilot's wheel and really had a ball piloting the ship. "I should really get into this kind of work in my next life," I jokingly told Jared. He smiled and stepped out onto the deck to smoke a cigarette.

The next day, I could see the Farasan Islands on the eastern horizon as we approached them. I figured they were about twelve miles away. Somewhere about noon, I was on the starboard side of the ship checking the cargo tie-downs because the sea was beginning to be a little rough. As I was doing my inspection, I noticed in the distance what seemed to be two or three small boats. I thought to myself that they probably wished they were somewhere else other than on the rough sea. While I watched, they were getting closer and closer to us. Finally, it looked as if they were coming to our ship. This seemed really strange to me.

After a few minutes, the three small boats, with five or six men in each, were alongside our ship. One of them yelled for permission to come aboard. Jared nodded "okay" and Raviv tossed a rope ladder over the edge of the ship. Soon, there were a dozen or so strangers on the ship's deck. I was somewhat shielded from them because of the cargo, but I could see enough to tell by their body language that Jared and one of the strangers were not in agreement.

Then, all of a sudden, I heard what sounded like gunshots! I quickly glanced around the cargo and saw that these invaders had repeat rifles and had shot several of the deckhands! I was stunned and crouched down behind the cargo crates. As I watched, they tossed the men they had shot overboard. Then they shot all of the other hands. Raviv tried to run only to be shot in the back. Finally, they walked up to Jared and held the rifle to his head. The leader said a few words in Arabic, paused, and then pulled the trigger. They shot Jared in cold blood and then tossed him overboard along with all the others. I had never been so frightened in my entire life.

I knew that if I was discovered, they would kill me also, so I used the crates as a blind and jumped off the ship into the water. I thought about floating on my back so I could breathe while giving the appearance that I was one of the floating dead, but I quickly dismissed that idea because my appearance was so drastically different from all the others. Instead, I went underwater and swam to the hull of the ship and tried to find something to grab hold of. Because of the overhang, I was shielded from the view of the deck. I figured if I could hang on for a while, the crew would stop combing the water, and maybe I'd have a chance to swim safely away. I was grateful that I had diving experience and had conditioned myself to hold my breath for some three to four minutes. If I could ease to the back of the ship and go underwater for four minutes, there should be a pretty good distance between me and the ship as it would be traveling away from me.

I couldn't believe that we had been high jacked by pirates! What did we have that they could possibly want? Then I had the chilling thought that maybe it was me! Did the government of Omen somehow find out about me and my mission and was trying to stop me? Could that be what Jared and the invaders were arguing about? Oh, what have I gotten myself into?

In addition to being scared out of my mind, I would truly miss Jared and Raviv and all of the other deckhands. I had learned to think of them as dear friends even though we couldn't communicate with each other very well. How sad to see all of them shot before my very eyes.

After hanging on for what seemed to be about five minutes, I began to hug the base of the ship as it slipped past me. When the back of the ship was near, I took a deep breath and dove beneath the surface of the water. I figured I was about ten feet deep when I began swimming away from the ship. I could clearly hear the engine noise and could tell that it was getting farther away. Finally, I needed a breath of air and shot to the surface and quickly took another breathe before submerging again. After another few minutes, I eased to the surface and the ship looked to be at least a hundred yards or so away from me, so I felt it was safe to stay above the water. Apparently, the pirates knew how to pilot the ship. I had really enjoyed Jared letting me do that.

Now, what was I to do? As I trod water, all I could see was water for miles and miles. I noted the direction the ship was headed and knew that it was headed south, which gave me a sense of direction. From observing the maps, I knew the closest land was to the east, so I began to swim. Again, I was grateful for being in pretty good shape and swimming was not a big burden for me, but to swim for some twenty miles was another story. I knew that I had to conserve strength, so I swam a while and then floated on my back for a while. This went on until dark. I was cold and scared and hungry. I prayed like I had never prayed before.

By this time, I was also getting thirsty and dehydrated, but the decision on what to do was simple. I had but one choice, which was to keep making my way eastward, but the problem was that I wasn't sure anymore if I was going east. I kept hoping to see a ship pass by, but none did. After swimming late into the night, I got a glimpse of some lights in the distance. I cannot explain what joyful hope that gave me. At least, there was a light at the end of the tunnel. This renewed hope gave me a fresh burst of energy. So, I swam and floated, swam and floated, and swam and floated.

Finally, I could see the dawning of the sun, and to my good fortune, it was indeed in front of me, which meant I had been going east.

I was exhausted, my muscles ached, and my body was weak. I wasn't sure if I could go very much farther. I found myself floating more than swimming. Fortunately for me, I was getting near enough to shore that the waves were increasing which drifted me closer and closer to land. About mid-morning, I glanced up and saw land in the near distance. I mustered up enough energy to swim some more and soon was in water shallow enough that I could stand and touch the bottom. Solid land had never felt so good as I waded out to the dry shore.

Obviously, I didn't know where I was, but the island appeared to be isolated. I glanced in all directions and there was no sign of life. Was I on one of the uninhabited islands, or was I in Saudi Arabia or Yemen? I had no idea. All I knew was that I was alive, for which I was thankful, and that I was thirsty, hungry, and exhausted. I noticed some palm trees just a bit inland. I thought I could go there and rest for a little while. If any people were around, they may be evil like the pirates, or they may be nice like the people in the Arizona Grand Canyon when I had the snake bite. All of that seemed like eons ago.

I sat down and leaned against the trunk of the largest tree and immediately went to sleep. When I woke up, the sun was well into the western sky which meant I had slept for at least five or six hours, maybe more. I was rested, but more than ever I had a craving for water, but where could I go to find some?

As I stood, my legs were weak, and I was wobbly. I knew that I couldn't walk very far in this condition, but I couldn't afford to stay where I was either. I decided to walk farther inland in hopes of finding a stream of some kind.

It wasn't long until the flat beach area gave way to some hills covered with scrubby little trees. As I stood on top of one of the hills, I could see the rugged terrain ahead of me. Surely there would be some kind of streams there, but I didn't think I could make it very far – yet there was really no other choice but to try.

I walked and walked through the brush and finally came to a clearing which made the walking a little easier. About midway through the clearing, I came across a well-traveled trail. Maybe this would lead me to some water, but which way should I go? I decided to go south, and after a short time, I became lightheaded and my surroundings began to turn around and around. I thought, "Is this it? Is this the way you feel just before you die?"

CHAPTER 10

I felt the heat from the sun on my face as I slowly opened my eyes. It took a few seconds for my focus to become clear, but once it did, I realized that I didn't know where I was. I noticed some small shelters nearby, but I saw no people. Things began to come back to me. I remembered the pirate invasion and my long swim to shore.

I remembered how thirsty I was and how weak I felt, but now I realized that my thirst was gone. Had I died and gone to heaven? Was I dead and my mind was playing games with me? I actually pinched myself, and to my surprise, it really hurt.

I also realized that I no longer had my wallet that contained all of my papers, my passport, and my money. Apparently, it was at the bottom of the sea somewhere. I had never felt so alone or lonely in my life. I had no idea what to do and realized that I could never get back to America without a passport.

I stood up and was looking around when I heard human voices in the distance, and it sounded as though they were coming in my direction. What was I to do? Should I run and hide? Lie down and pretend to be sleeping? Or should I stand and face whoever might appear? I decided to stand my ground.

Soon, three people came into sight. There was an older man and two younger boys who I assumed were his sons. They were herding a flock of goats, but when they saw me, they seemed delighted to see that I was up and standing. They left the goats and came over to me. They acted friendly and showed compassion toward me. Although they were not speaking English, I could tell by their hand motions that they were asking if I was hungry. I indicated that I was. So, they motioned that I follow them.

They led me around some of the buildings to a primitive looking house. It reminded me of the "Little House on the Prairie." The best I could tell, there was no electricity anywhere. I followed them inside where I saw several women. One appeared to be the mother and three younger girls that I guessed to be daughters. The oldest of the three girls spoke English and asked me if I was hungry. I told her that I was and was thirsty also. She offered me a glass of milk, which I assumed to be goat milk and a plate of what looked to be stew. I wasn't sure what it was, but it tasted delicious.

After eating, I talked with the girl and asked her name. She said it was Anis, which meant friendly. I told her that was a very pretty name and was certainly fitting for her. I told her my name was Sonny.

She asked how I was feeling and I told her much better, and then I asked her where we were and how long I had been here. She told me that I was on an island called Jabel-Reed and that her brothers found me about four days ago. I gathered from what she said, I was unconscious for those days. Naturally, she wanted to know where I came from, and I told her that I was from the United States and was working on a cargo ship that was hijacked and how I escaped and swam to shore. She said there was a lot of pirating in the Red Sea lately and most of it was politically motivated.

I asked her where she learned to speak English so well. She said she attended the University of Cairo and had the opportunity to attend Duke University in North Carolina as a medical exchange student. I was stunned at what she said and wondered why a medical student would be living on a remote island such as this. She told me that both her parents became ill and she dropped out of school to come back home and look after them. "Fortunately, they are both much better now, but I haven't returned to my studies," she said.

The more Anis talked, the more I was impressed with her, not to mention her beautiful natural olive complexion, dark hair, and brown eyes. I asked her age and she said she was twenty-seven. I was surprised as she looked to be a teenager.

We talked for a long time, and then the reality of my mission came to mind and I wondered how I was going to get to Aden, Yemen, and how I was going to meet up with Nadir. If I missed him, how could I pull off my rescue mission? I asked Anis how far we were from Aden and how I could get there. She said she wasn't sure how far it was, but that it would be difficult to get there from here.

She said the problem is that their island is in a Saudi Arabian province which disallows any travelers in or out of Yemen without extreme scrutiny. She said, "We are about fifteen miles from Jizan, Saudi Arabia. There is a coastline highway that goes to Aden from there, but without proper credentials, you would not be allowed to enter Yemen. You can't just go there freely from here. Do you have business there?"

I told her that I was supposed to meet some people there and now it looked as though I would miss my meeting. I wanted to tell her of my mission in hopes that she might be able to help, but should I? Surely, her being isolated the way she is and the circumstance by which we met could not have been staged. I felt I could trust her but thought it best not to mention this to her just yet.

I asked her how large this island is, and she said it was only about twenty square miles and was smaller than most of the ones in the area. Next, I asked how many miles it was to the Yemen coast. I was thinking I might be able to swim that far if I had some food and water provisions, but when she said probably at least sixty miles, I dismissed that idea.

Then I asked if there were any boats I could use for the trip. She said the only boats they had were small fishing boats and they were not really seaworthy. Then she added, "Once a week, a government cruiser comes from Jizan to all the islands and ferries people to the mainland and then brings them back that same afternoon. This is how the government keeps control of the people."

I asked her if I would be allowed to ride that ferry, and she said we probably could. I picked up on the word "we" but let it slide for now. Then she walked across the room and got something out of a cabinet drawer. When she returned, she handed me my wallet.

"Here you are, Sonny Scroggins. When we found you, we were searching for identification and discovered all the papers in your wallet were wet, so I took them all out and dried them in the sun and then replaced them where I thought they belonged. You might double-check." I don't think I have ever been as happy to receive anything as I was this wallet!

I thumbed through it, and things looked to be in order. I especially checked my passport. Other than having a few of the letters smeared, it looked to be okay and was certainly readable. My picture and name were still clear.

After visiting with Anis, she asked if I'd like a tour of their place. I welcomed her invitation, so we started walking. There were several outbuildings serving as barns and storage, and she explained to me that her parents had lived on this island all their lives and raising goats was their manner of livelihood.

They milked the goats and sold the milk and cheese to people on the mainland. "So, the weekly ferry is our delivery wagon. Once in Jizan, Papa has a booth where he sets up, and regular customers come by every week and buy from him. We don't make very much money, but it is an honest living". I loved hearing her talk because

she not only spoke fluent English, but she had an Arabian accent....
or some kind of accent.....that I assumed to be Arabian. I suspect my
East Texas accent was also new to her.

I asked how her dad kept the milk from spoiling and she said
they have a water-tight container that allows them to lower the milk
into a water well which maintains about a forty-degree temperature.
I was favorably impressed.

Then she took me to see some of the grazing lands which
seemed to have an ample supply of grass not to mention all the scrub
timber that was everywhere. One thing I noticed was that there were
no fences, and she explained that it was all open range. She said there
were only three other families living on the island, so the open range
concept was not a problem.

The more I listened to her, the more this slow-paced way of life
had its appeal. When we made our way to the beach area, I noticed
that it was really beautiful. The beach had white clean sand and the
water was blue. I tried very hard to spot some ocean liners in the
distance, but if there were any, they were too far out for me to see.

As the sun settled in the western sky, Anis said we needed to get
back to the house as it was about time for the evening milking. She
said I was welcome to observe if I'd like. I told her that I certainly
would like it.

The goats were like cattle back home. They each had a separate
stall where they were fed, and Anis' father and two brothers were
busy milking ten goats. Once the milk pail was filled, they handed
it to one of the girls who poured it into what looked to be a plastic
container that resembled a large handbag. When the container was
full, they clamped a seal on the top and attached it to a rope and lowered it into a nearby well that had an opening about six feet across. It
was certainly large enough to accommodate a lot of these milk bags.

It was dark by the time the work was done, and then we all gathered for an evening meal. Although I could not understand the words,

I was very pleased that Anis' dad led a prayer before the meal. I didn't know if he was praying to "our God" or to Buddha or what, but I would ask Anis later. Her parents were delightful and gracious hosts.

As the evening progressed, I became concerned about where I was to sleep. In all the looking around, I had seen no bedrooms. Finally, it was bedtime, and everyone got up to leave the main house.

Anis took my hand and told me to come with her. She took me to one of the buildings outside. She pointed to one and said that was her parents' sleeping quarters. Then she pointed to another and said that was where her brothers slept. Finally, she pointed to the one next door and said that was the girl's dorm and where she would be sleeping. She continued to say the building behind where we were standing was the guest house and where I would stay. Then she added that they didn't have beds like we do in America so everyone slept on bedding on the ground. I thought that a bit strange, but it was fine with me.

That night as I was lying on the bedding, I didn't know what I was to do. I felt sure that Nadir was no longer waiting for me, and without that contact, I was pretty helpless. I had very little money and no way to get off this island. I should have stayed in Texas, but I had to admit, it was a real blessing to meet Anis and I certainly enjoyed her company.

I was confident that God had been with me throughout this ordeal, or else I would have been shot like the others on the ship, and I never would have made it to an island where someone could speak English. I believed that if God had brought me this far, He wouldn't forsake me now. Just before I went to sleep, I decided I needed to solicit help from Anis. She seemed knowledgeable and spoke of family honesty. Tomorrow, I would fill her in on my mission. Then my thoughts shifted back to home and Kali, and I wondered if they were worried about me. I knew for sure that Mom was.

The next morning everyone was up early and went through the milking process again. This time I helped them gather to feed and place it in the troughs in the goat stalls. I realized that as long as I was staying here, I should do my share of the work, which I enjoyed doing.

Anis laughed at me as I struggled to get the feed into the troughs faster than the goats could eat it. After the milking was finished, she told me that later I could go with her brothers to lead the goats out to the grazing land where we would stay with them to protect them from predators. I asked her what kind of predators there were on such a small island. She said, "The two-legged kind. People will come in by boat and steal goats either for themselves or to sell at the market."

Before I headed out with her brothers, I told Anis that I needed a few minutes to talk with her alone. She said we could get together to talk in the afternoon after the goats were brought back to the house. I tagged along with the guys and really enjoyed the peace and tranquility of nature. We couldn't communicate with each other verbally, but we did well with sign language.

I observed several species of birds and a few chipmunk-looking critters. I supposed they could be found all over the world. When we returned from the grazing land in the afternoon, I had a chance to walk with Anis to the beach area that I thought was so beautiful. It was really a very romantic setting.

We sat down on the beach, and I told her all about my mission and why it was so important for me to get to Aden, although I now feared it was too late. Besides, I didn't know what Nadir looked like. She seemed to be amazed at what I was trying to accomplish and impressed by my loyalty to my friend. I told her that I was beginning to second-guess my judgment in trying to pull off the rescue.

Finally, she reached over and took my hand and looked into my eyes as she said, "Sonny, I'll do whatever I can to help you." I thanked her and the moment seemed right to lean over and kiss her. She welcomed my advancement by wrapping her arms around my neck in a tight embrace as we both slowly sat down on the white sandy beach.

After a short time of cuddling, she said we needed to get back. As we walked, I asked her again about the road into Yemen. I was wondering if I could get near the border and then make my way out into the sea far enough to swim past the border and to the Yemen shore. She said she didn't know but it might work. Tomorrow was the day to go to the mainland, and maybe we could check it out. We held hands as we made our way back to the house, and I was beginning to really like and trust Anis.

That night, after I went to bed, I was trying to "think everything through" as I had been taught to do since childhood. As Armand put it, it was time for me to improvise. While I was lying there, to my surprise Anis slipped in and quietly came over to where I was. She leaned down and said, "I wanted to tell you good night in my own special way." Then she seemingly melted into my arms. Things seemed so right with her. I had absolutely no doubts about her trustworthiness like I had with Kali. She stayed with me for quite a while and we whispered sweet nothings to each other. Finally, she got up and said, "Good night and sweet dreams" and then left.

I was about to lose the focus of my mission because I was beginning to want to spend the rest of my life isolated on this island with Anis and her family.

The next morning, we were up early and finished our chores before breakfast. After eating, all the milk containers were gathered and placed in a cart pulled by one of the larger goats. I wasn't sure where we were going, but I tagged along and talked with Anis all the way. After a short time, we were at a dock by the sea. We didn't have to wait very long before the shuttle ferry arrived, and we all loaded up except for one brother who took the goat and cart back to the house.

After about an hour, or maybe a little less, we were in Jizan. I was impressed with the city. It was modern with a population of more than a half million people. There were open markets all along the port side with all kinds of tropical fruits and agricultural produce. Anis' father led us to his market booth where there were refrigerators to keep the milk and cheese fresh. Once he was set up, Anis and I left to try to find a place to rent a car.

She used the telephone book and found a rental place not too far from the dock area. As we were walking to the lot, I spotted a McDonalds a few blocks down the street. I was surprised to see one over here, and it really made me hungry for an American hamburger, but we didn't stop. We rented a car for the day and headed down the Saudi Freeway which followed the coastline toward Yemen.

After about forty miles, we could see the traffic slow down as we neared the border where there were traffic checks. I turned around and began to look for some roads that looked like they would lead to the beach. I found one that took us directly to the beach, and then it turned and followed the beach back toward Jizan. I noted the road number as we stopped at an isolated part of the beach and walked down to the water's edge. I figured I might be able to enter the water somewhere along here, and after a five- or six-hour swim, I should be in Yemen.

Anis was supportive of me but asked a very sobering question. "What are you going to do once you get to Yemen? You are going to be on foot with no idea where to go, and you will also be dripping wet and you can't speak their language." She was right, so I began to rethink that idea. Then she suggested that we try to get through customs as a couple doing something. That way we would at least have a car. I liked that idea better if we could pull it off.

When we got back to the car, a police car pulled up behind us with its lights flashing. I didn't know what to expect, but I feared I might be arrested for driving without a Saudi Arabian license. We would soon find out as the officer got out of his car and headed our way.

CHAPTER 11

As the officer approached, he had a stern look on his face and his demeanor was one that showed a serious no-nonsense personality. He glanced at the license plate on our car and jotted something down on his notepad. Then he walked over to us. As I expected, he said something in Arabic, and I assumed he was asking to see my driver's license. Immediately, before I had time to say a word, Anis spoke up and handed him her license. He looked at it and then asked what we were doing. She told me later that she said I was a guest visiting from America and she was showing me the sites. Then in English, she asked, "Officer, have we done anything wrong?"

Before answering her, he asked in English to see my passport. I handed it to him, and he looked at it for a long time. This really made me nervous. Finally, he gave it back to me and said, "Mr. Scroggins, have a good visit in our country."

Then he turned to Anis and said, "No, I guess you did nothing wrong. I noticed that you did a u-turn back on the turnpike which looked a little suspicious, and then when you turned onto the feeder road, I thought I should check it out." He handed Anis her license back and apologized for any inconvenience he might have caused us.

As he got back into his car, my heart rate settled just a little while I moved to the passenger side of the car and let Anis drive. I told her that it never occurred to me to let her drive as I was so accustomed to always getting behind the wheel. She said she had no problem with me driving unless we get checked. We now laughed at the incident, but I was so grateful that she had a legal license in spite of not having a car. She said several years ago, her parents sent her to a boarding school on the Mainland where she received her education. While there, all the students who were of age were encouraged to get their driver's license, which she did. Since then, she had continued to renew it and keep it current.

Later that day, we returned the car to the rental agency and made our way back to the marketplace. We noticed that the ferryboat had just left! We could see it in the near distance of the harbor, but we missed it. We would have been back in plenty of time to catch it if the policeman had not detained us. Now, what were we to do? I had very little money, and what I had was in Egyptian currency. Once again I realized that we needed to improvise.

Anis didn't know of any way to get to her island, and especially this late in the day. She said maybe tomorrow we could find a fisherman who might take us back. But for now, we were stranded. My thought was, "I couldn't think of anyone I had rather be stranded with," but I kept that thought to myself.

We sat on the dock trying to decide what to do. I asked her how far away the airport was. She said, "A good ways, why?"

I told her that I had frequently slept on the sofas in airport terminals and that they are much more comfortable than sleeping on the street. She said it was too far to walk, but a bus station was just a few blocks away. I told her that would probably work just as well.

When we got to the bus station, it was packed with people, but soon three buses loaded up which reduced the crowd number dramatically. Anis showed me a place in the bus station where I could get my money converted into local currency, which would really help out. After that we went to their snack bar and grabbed a sandwich, and while we were eating, we discussed ways I might be able to cross into Yemen.

While we were talking, I saw a magazine rack and noticed one entitled *Travel*. I suggested that we pose as a photography team taking pictures for a travel magazine. I asked Anis what kind of credentials she thought we would need in order to do that. She said we would probably need passports, which we both had, and some kind of company identification along with some camera equipment.

I asked her if she had any contacts who might be able to help us. She thought for a minute but couldn't come up with anyone. I asked if she knew anyone at her school who had an interest in photography. Again, she came up empty, but said, "Maybe my school marshal, who is what you would call a superintendent, might be able to help us." We agreed to go to the school first thing tomorrow.

Then I stunned her when I asked if she knew where I could rent a helicopter. With a chuckle, she quickly replied, "Absolutely not! I wouldn't know where to even begin to get a helicopter. I guess you are going to tell me that you know how to fly one." I smiled and said, "Yep."

I went over to the magazine rack and bought a copy of *Travel*. I thought the photography idea might work for us, but what I was really interested in was the company logo that was printed on the back cover. If we could somehow scan that logo and use it as a backdrop for a company photo ID, the plan might work.

While we were looking at the magazine, Anis noticed the bus departure schedule and said one of them went to Aden, Yemen. I asked her if we could cross the border on the bus. She thought perhaps we could if we had the proper credentials.

Later, we freshened up in the restrooms and then made our way to the lounge area where we watched a little television before we settled down for the night.

The next morning, we went to Anis' old school and visited with her school marshal. He told us that one of her classmates had a photoshop in the city and would be glad to visit with us.

When we got to the fella's shop, he recognized Anis right away and seemed delighted to see her, but he appeared a little suspicious of me. She explained to him that I was her friend from America and that I really needed to get to Aden but was having trouble getting through customs. He was fully aware of the complication of getting into Yemen. He wanted to know what we needed and seemed more than willing to help so long as his name or store was never mentioned.

We agreed. He snapped our picture and had the technology to scan the *Travel* logo and edit it to include our pictures. When he finished, we each had a laminated badge that looked official. I don't think Robert or Janet could have done any better. Before we left, he provided us with some old inoperable cameras. It would help our case, and he planned to get rid of them anyway. Now it seemed we were set with a plan.

The next order of business was to try to catch a ride back to her island. By early afternoon, we were back at the dock trying to find a fisherman who would give us a lift. Most of the fishermen were just returning from their days run and were busy cleaning their catch. I was beginning to think we would need to spend another night at the bus station, but Anis finally found a friend of her family who agreed to take us back. I offered him some fuel money, but he refused and said it was a favor for their friendship.

When we arrived, Anis' family was glad to see us as they had been very concerned since they didn't know where we were or if we were safe. She explained how we just barely missed the ferry and spent the night at the bus station. Then she told them she needed to go and help me with a project that might take several days and that they shouldn't worry about her being gone too long. Obviously, they were not too keen on the idea, but recognizing Anis' determination, they agreed. It pleased me to know they trusted me enough to allow me to take their daughter away from her home for a few days. After all, I was basically a stranger from a foreign land to them.

We had to wait another week before we could return to the Mainland. That would give us time to plan our strategy, and I would enjoy the peaceful time spent with Anis. I resumed doing my chores during that week and got much better and proficient at feeding the goats. The relationship between Anis and me deepened and I felt blessed.

The week passed, and we were once again on the Mainland. Anis had a little money that she had saved, and with what I had, we bought bus tickets to Aden. Soon, we were aboard and heading south toward Yemen. All the while, I felt uneasy, and as I held Anis' hand, she had sweaty palms-- so I knew that she was nervous also.

When we made it to the border, buses were directed to a special lane where each passenger was asked to leave the bus and go into a building for interrogation. After we were unloaded, the border patrols inspected the bus.

As they talked to people before us, some of them were allowed to get back on the bus, but a few were taken into custody and taken somewhere else. Then it was our turn. We each showed them our passports. I guess it looked odd to them that a Saudi and an American were traveling together.

We explained that we were going into Yemen as part of the photography team for *Travel Magazine.* I showed them the magazine copy that I had, and we both showed our ID badges. They glanced at the badges and looked at the camera cases we each had strapped across our shoulders. They asked why we didn't fly into Aden. Anis said that we were asked to photograph some rural areas within Yemen as well as the resorts in Aden, and riding the bus made it much easier to do that.

Our interrogating officer walked away for a minute to confer with another officer. I feared they were going to call *Travel Magazine* to verify our employment. Again, my heart raced although I was trying to remain calm. In a short time, the officer returned and stamped our bus ticket and motioned for us to get back on the bus. What a relief that was! We both had to work really hard to control our emotions inside the office, but when we got back on the bus, we both giggled like children.

Finally, the bus was back on the road, and we were in the country of Yemen headed for the city of Aden. It was about a fifteen-hour ride, but we finally arrived. After getting off the bus, neither of us knew anything about Aden and certainly didn't know where to go. It was a few hours before daylight and my suggestion was to stay at the bus station until daylight and then go to the seaport where I was originally supposed to dock and maybe we could find a clue. Like in Gibraltar, I bought a city map to help us find the dock. It wasn't too far from the bus station, so in order to save our money, we decided to walk. Before leaving the bus station, we again had our money converted to Yemen currency, and while we were doing that, a news flash came on the television that said, "Earlier today, there was a bombing in the Jizan, Yemen, bus station and seven people were killed with dozens more injured. Early speculation is that it was done by a radical terrorist group."

My legs became weak. We both sat down on a nearby couch and were shocked at what we were hearing. Just a few hours earlier, we were in that station. Then the thought again occurred to me as I said, "Anis, do you think that was an attempt to stop me?" With a look of fear on her face, she said she didn't know. Since we were stopped by the police officer who spent a lot of time looking at my passport, he knew I was in the area and alive. Perhaps, spies were watching us and planned an assassination attack. Finally, I got control of my imagination and convinced myself that I was just being paranoid and that it was probably just a coincidence that the bombing took place where I had been. Once again, I wondered if the attack on the ship by the pirates had been meant for me.

When we got our money, we walked down to the wharf area to snoop around. As we were looking, to my amazement I spotted the Libertine ship docked there. I quickly pointed it out to Anis and told her that was the ship I had been on. I wondered if that was the dock where Nadir was expecting to meet me. I wondered too if the crew on board was the pirates who hijacked us. As I watched from a distance, I didn't recognize any of the crew that was on deck because all of the ones I knew had been killed.

I asked Anis for advice as to what I should do. She didn't have any other than to not let those deckhands see me. I agreed as we tried to slip into obscurity where we could watch. As we watched, we talked about what we were going to do if we saw something of interest and where we were going to stay while in Aden. We agreed that maybe we could stay in the bus station again unless someone ran us off.

As we were softly talking, a dignified man walked out of the captain's office of the ship, left the ship, and started walking in our direction. I wondered if it was Nadir. And if it was, why he was talking with the hijackers unless he was really a bad guy working against my mission. If that was true, I was fortunate that I didn't hook up with him.

I told Anis that I had more questions now than ever before. I really didn't know who to trust, if anyone, with the exception of her. She leaned over and kissed my cheek and told me that she was my soulmate. I wasn't sure what that meant, but it sounded good, and I liked it.

As the stranger got to the street, an expensive-looking car picked him up and drove off. Before he got into the car, he was close enough to us that we both got a good look at him.

I told Anis that I wanted to go to the Mecure Hotel. Jared mentioned it as if he was implying that was where I could meet Nadir. We found it on the map and headed in that direction. After a bit, we approached a luxurious resort with a beautiful hotel that was surrounded by beautiful pools and gardens. We were dressed casually with our camera cases, so we looked to be tourists and should not arouse suspicion as we wandered around.

We walked through the lobby area but did not see our stranger. Next, we checked out the lounges and bars but still came up empty. After we walked around for a while, we sat in the lobby watching people come in and out. I was fascinated by watching people who appeared to be the rich and famous come and go at will. Finally, I spotted our man getting off of the elevator! I pointed him out to Anis and whispered, "Now what?"

She whispered back, "Just sit back and watch." She got up and went across the lobby and approached the elevator where our mystery man was standing. She then backed into him as if it was an accident. Then in Arabic, I assumed she was apologizing to him for being so careless. I could tell that she was really pouring on the charm, and he was falling victim to her advances. I heard her give him a name that wasn't hers, and in return, he said his name was Nadir. After exchanging room numbers, Anis got on the elevator and went up to some other floor.

I watched as Nadir stared at her while she was getting on the elevator. Soon, a man who appeared to be his driver came in and they both left. As soon as they left the building, Anis came back to where I was and said, "You're right! He is your man!"

Now I was worried all the more that I was being set up by Kali and Armand, but why? We left the hotel to avoid the further risk of being detected and made our way back to the bus station. We found an isolated part of the station lobby where we sat and talked. I told Anis that I still felt compelled more than ever to try to make the rescue, but we would have to make it alone without the help of the Oman government; in fact, maybe in spite of the Omen government. As we talked, we mapped out a plan as to how we might do it on our own.

CHAPTER 12

After a brief rest, we had a few hours before dark and decided to go check out the rental of scuba equipment. There were several shops in close proximity of us that were near the shipyard. As we approached the first shop, I was very surprised to see Nadir's car drive up and park in front of the store! More surprising than that, Armand got out of the car and went inside!

He had some papers in his hand that from our distance looked as if they had pictures on them. I grabbed Anis and pulled her over behind the corner of a building across the street. She also recognized the car we had seen Nadir in earlier, but she didn't know Armand. I whispered to her that he was the man I had met in the library back home and who gave me the few instructions I had about making this trip. Now for sure, I felt that my life was in jeopardy! Could I not trust anyone? Soon, Armand came out of the scuba shop and got into the car and they drove off.

I figured it was not safe for me to go into the store, so I gave instructions to Anis and sent her in to get prices to rent equipment. In a few minutes, she returned with the prices and said she saw a copy of my picture lying on top of the counter. We figured that

Armand and Nadir were getting the word out to scuba shops that if I showed up, they should be notified.

Now I also knew that it was not safe for me to be walking the streets, so we headed back to the bus station and found a secluded place where we could watch the entrance. I wondered if I needed to buy a wig and some other forms of disguise.

I sent Anis to buy a Yemen state map. I couldn't remember exactly where the Grand Canyon area was but knew the approximate location. I suggested that tomorrow we go to the farmers market and try to find a farmer from that area who might give us a lift back to his farm with the disguised intent of taking some rural pictures for the *Travel Magazine.*

The next morning, we took a taxi to the farmers' market which was about a mile from the shipyard where the Libertine was docked. Anis spoke to the merchants in Arabic and asked them where they lived and grew their produce. It wasn't long until we found a man who lived on the coastal plains near the region where we wanted to go. She explained to him that we wanted to take some rural pictures and his farm sounded like the perfect spot for us. Then she asked if he would be so kind as to let us ride with him back to his farm later that afternoon. He was overwhelmed with excitement at the idea that his farm might be in a nationally distributed magazine and graciously agreed that we could ride with him.

We returned to the marketplace in the early afternoon and helped the farmer load his produce that did not sell, and then the three of us crowded into his pickup truck. It took us about an hour and a half to get to his farm, and we arrived a couple of hours before dark. He introduced us to his wife and kids. They were all very cordial and excited, and I felt bad that we were deceiving them. I was amazed at the trust he seemed to have in us.

We played our role perfectly as we walked around and pretended to be snapping some pictures. We even staged a few poses.

Eventually, Anis asked about the mountains in the near background. The man began to tell her about them and how dangerous they were. In the course of the conversation, she asked about the region called "the Grand Canyon."

He pointed and said the mouth of the canyon was just around the ridge to our left. It was about ten miles away. She asked if he would drive us there tomorrow, and he was very willing to do so. In the meanwhile, they treated us like royalty and even gave us their bedroom. We accepted their hospitality, and I respected Anis's purity and slept on the floor while she had the bed. I would have enjoyed spending more time with this family.

The next morning, before he drove back to Aden, the farmer took us to the river that flowed from the middle of the great canyon. I felt strongly that somewhere up ahead my friend Ron and Tim were being held against their will. I felt that I was very close to finding them. I guess I had a woman's intuition even though I was a man.

The river was rather wide and slow-moving, which implied that the water was deep, but I knew that was not the case for very far. I told Anis that all I knew to do was start hiking upstream. Fortunately, the farming couple packed us a sack lunch, but that would not sustain us for the long haul. I anticipated this and had Anis ask the farmer if he had a small amount of rope and a fishing line with a hook that he could spare. He did, and I tucked it down inside my camera case.

As we hiked up the river, it didn't take long until we got into some very rugged terrain. The river narrowed and became very swift. The bank area of the river narrowed and was lined with very slippery rocks. I held to Anis's hand to try to prevent her from falling. I could tell we would not be able to continue this course, so I began looking for a place where we could climb up the mountain so we could travel above the river. We walked back down the river until we found a place where we could climb to the top of the hill. I was concerned about Anis because all of this was a new experience for her, but she was a real trooper and didn't complain a single time. I liked her more and more and realized my feelings were deeper than "liking".

Once on top, we took a much-needed lunch break. I didn't know what kind of sandwiches we ate, but they were very satisfying to a growling stomach. After resting for a while, we continued our hike. The terrain here was not much easier than down on the river. I remembered from studying the topographical maps that these mountains became very rugged before we could get to the facility where I thought Tim and Ron were held captive. We were doing all of this based on a hunch which seemed absurd when I thought about it!

After a few hours of hiking, I called it off. I told Anis that there had to be a better way. Now I understood the need for a helicopter. If only things had gone as planned, the mission might have been completed by now. Instead, I was having to improvise in a strange land where I could not speak the language, and I also might be putting Anis's life in danger.

I told her I was so thankful, in more ways than one, that she had come into my life. She smiled and said, "Me too." She said she considered this to be a great adventure and that she had always enjoyed doing new things. More and more I could see myself spending the rest of my life with her.

After discussing our options, we decided to leave the mountains and return to Aden and try to locate a helicopter. Darkness was going to overtake us before we could make our way back to the coastline, so we had to make a camp. I was glad the farmer and his wife didn't expect us to come back to their house that night, or else they would have been concerned about our whereabouts.

I thought I would tease Anis by asking her how we were going to build a fire. She said she didn't know other than rubbing sticks together. I had bought a pocketknife and cigarette lighter while we were at the bus station in Aden, but she didn't know I had them.

Then I pulled out the lighter and said, "What about using this?" She slugged me on my forearm and said, "You tease! You had me worried!"

Gathering firewood was not a problem as it was all around us in abundance, and the lighter really came in handy to start the fire. Soon, we had a good hot fire burning. I had selected a place for the campsite that was surrounded on three sides by rocks, so we were in an area that was protected from strong winds or predators, and we had the reflective heat and light from the fire. As I suspected, once the sun went down, it became quite cold and neither of us was dressed for the cold.

As the darkness of the night overshadowed us, we were cuddled by the warmth of the fire. Both of us were hungry but had nothing to eat. I told her if we continued to stay in the mountains, I would build a snare with the rope the farmer gave us and try to catch some fish. I assured her that we would survive, but now that we were on our way out, we would just have to be hungry until tomorrow.

As we sat near the fire, Anis snuggled into my arms and asked me to tell her about East Texas. I began by describing my home and family. I told her that I had three siblings who were triplets and numerous cousins. We were all remarkably close and looked forward to spending time together. I tried to describe the terrain and the lifestyle to her.

I also told her that we had several law-enforcement people in our family along with some medical professionals and special investigators. Then I told her the story of Little Pete and his battle against polio. I thought she would be interested in that since she had been a medical student. However, she didn't know what polio was until I told her. Then she said, "Sonny, it sounds like a very lovely place. I can hardly wait to get there."

I wondered what she meant by that. Did she want to visit, or was it much deeper than that — like permanently as my wife? I kept my thoughts to myself, but a lifetime with Anis would be just fine with me as I knew for sure that I loved and cared about her. But did I love her enough to make a lifetime commitment with her?

Then she asked me about my religion. I told her about the church and what and why I believed what I did. She told me that she grew up Muslim but really was not committed to that belief. She said there were a lot of things about that belief with which she struggled. I told her that I was pleased to see her parents pray at mealtime, but I didn't know to whom they were praying since I couldn't understand what they were saying.

I told her that I wasn't as committed to following the Bible as I knew I should be, but I planned to be more faithful when, or if, I got back home. I told her I knew God had protected me all along this journey.

Then she asked me my view on children and how many I would like to have. As I ran my fingers through her dark brown hair while staring at the flicker of the fire, I asked her why she asked that. She said she was just curious and wanted to know how I felt about some of the things that mattered to her in life. I told her that I hadn't ever thought about that before, but I thought a nice family size would be two to four children. Then she squeezed my arm tightly and said, "Me too."

We went to sleep in each other's arms and kept warm from the fire and reflective heat off the rocks. Several times throughout the night, I got up and put more wood on the fire, but had no problem going back to sleep. The last time I got up, after rekindling the fire, I looked at Anis as she slept near the fire. She was so beautiful outwardly, but she was just as beautiful on the inside as out.

We enjoyed doing so many of the same things. I would love to introduce her to east Texas, but I wasn't sure I was ready for that. Then as I lay back down, I thought about home and my eyes filled with tears as I missed everyone. I knew how worried about me Mom and Dad would be as well as all my other relatives. I wished I had some way to contact them. I also missed Scottie and Fuzzy.

The next morning, we were up early and left the campsite. All the way down the mountain, I kept thinking about the conversations Anis and I had. I couldn't shake the feelings I had for her. We finally made our way back to the river's edge. I gave her the lighter and asked her to build a fire while I tried my hand at fishing. I knew back home if you uncovered an old rotten log, there would likely be some grub worms or some kind of bug you could use for bait. I soon rolled over a decaying log, and sure enough, there were some kind of worms which I snatched up and soon had it out into the river.

While I fished, nothing happened. I found a calm place in the river that was protected from the swift currents and looked to me that it would be a good fishing spot, but nothing. After my patience wore thin, I cut a small sapling for a fishing pole and tied my fishing line to the end of it. I tossed the bait out into the swift water, and right away a fish took it and almost yanked the pole out of my hand.

It was quite a tussle, but I finally got him on the bank, and we soon had him roasting over the fire. I don't know what kind of fish it was, but beyond a doubt, it was the best I had ever eaten.

A few hours later, we were back on the road and ready for our ten-mile hike back to the produce farmer's place. After walking a few miles, as luck would have it, we met him coming toward us in his pickup truck. He said he was coming to check on us for which we were very thankful. I returned his rope and fishing line and hook to him, and we nodded to each other in gratitude. As we arrived back at the farmhouse, Anis asked if we could ride back with him to Aden the next morning, and he graciously agreed.

When we arrived in Aden the next day with the farmer, we took a cab to the airport where I began my search for helicopter service. I was glad Anis could read the telephone book which showed a few to be near the airport, but I couldn't find them. Anis finally went to a car rental agent and asked a young man for directions.

He told her the helicopter rental company was located in the back of a hanger on the other side of the runway. He added that it was hard to find, so we needed to look very closely. Anis kindly asked him if he might drive us over there during his break. Her charm worked once again, and after a few minutes, he motioned for us to follow him as he led us to a rental car and quickly drove us to the helicopter place. As he had said, there was only a small sign that said, "Aviation Rental" located above the hanger door, and we would probably have missed seeing it. We thanked him for the ride and gave him a tip for his help.

Anis and I went inside the hanger and found an older man seated behind a disarrayed counter. I asked if he spoke English, and he replied, "a little." I asked him what kind of helicopters he had and how much it would cost to rent one. He told me he had Robinson R22's and R44's.

Since I had used the R44 when I flew to the Grand Canyon in Arizona and was familiar with it, I specified that one. He told me that he rented those for $125 per hour, $500 per day or $2500 per week. I asked him how many he had available. When I asked that question, he excused himself, went to an office and made a telephone call. When he returned, he said he had four available and ready to go and a fifth one should be ready later in the day.

I guess he recognized that I was serious as he opened up and started telling me about the success of the helicopter and how he rented many of them to oil companies that flew to the well sites. After a long dialog and history lesson on the R44, I was able to break loose and leave. I told him that Anis and I needed to discuss it plus I needed to arrange for some other supplies as well.

When we walked back outside, we were welcomed by some strangers that had gotten out of Nadir's car! They grabbed me and forced me into the car. Inside was Nadir and Armand. The last thing I saw as we drove away was Anis struggling with two of their muscle men! Armand said to me, "Hello, Mr. Scroggins, we need to talk."

CHAPTER 13

Being forced into the backseat of a car with dark tinted windows between Armand and Nadir was one of the most terrifying experiences of my life! I knew at some point I was going to be shot in the head like Jared and dumped somewhere in an isolated area of Yemen.

Instantly my thoughts reflected on home and family. They would never know what happened to me other than what Scottie knew. They would never know of Anis, and I would never know what happened to her. At that instant, I was fully aware of how much I cared about her. My flashing reflections were interrupted by Armand saying, "Mr. Scroggins, we have been looking for you."

"Really!" I replied. "So you can kill me like you killed Jared?"

"Jared is dead?" Armand asked and seemed genuinely surprised.

"Of course he is dead! Your hit men took care of him and all of his crew. Now I suppose you plan to take care of me also," I replied.

"Oh no, no, no! You don't understand! We want to help you!"

Sarcastically, I said, "Right! Help me do what?"

Then Armand introduced me to Nadir who, like Armand, spoke perfect English. "Mr. Scroggins, apparently you misunderstand. We are not here to harm you; we still want to help you in your rescue mission. When you failed to arrive on the Libertine Ship, we distributed pictures of you all around town where we thought you may go in an attempt to find you. When the Libertine docked, I went aboard to meet my dear friend Jared, but someone else that I did not know was running the ship. He said Jared got sick at the Suez Canal and asked him to deliver his cargo. I had no idea until now that Jared was dead."

I was shocked at what I was hearing! I had assumed they were looking for me to kill me while all the time they wanted to help me. I apologized to them and explained the reason for my distrust. They were sorry to hear about Jared and his crew. It was becoming apparent to them that the attack on the ship was indeed an attempt to get me. Somehow, the purpose of my mission had leaked out. I kept my thoughts to myself, but my immediate suspect was Kali. But if that was the case, why did she send Armand to me to try to help me? My feelings for her had always been conflicting.

Armand said he came to Yemen when he received word that the ship had arrived and that I was not on it. Nadir could not recognize me, so Armand came to help find me. I asked him where he got my picture, and he simply said it wasn't hard with all the public records available in my country.

Then I told them about Anis and how she was helping me and that she needed to be protected. They assured me that she would not be harmed by their people. That was a great relief to me.

Finally, we drove up to the Mecure Hotel Resort where I was escorted up to their room. As we walked inside, the first thing I saw was Anis. She ran over to me and gave me a big Texas-sized hug. She said, "Oh, Sonny! I was afraid I would never see you again."

"Me too," I replied. I told her how much I feared never seeing her again and how much I realized that I cared for her. Then I said, "Anis, we misread the intentions of these men. They were trying to find me to help us, not harm us. We may still be able to get what we need to complete my mission."

Nadir interrupted us and said, "Mr. Scroggins, tomorrow we will meet in this room and make plans for your mission. But for now, you and your charming lady friend need some rest. You have both had several tough days. We have rented the room across the hall where you can rest and recuperate. I expect each of you would welcome a hot shower."

I had to admit that a shower sounded wonderful. I tried to think back to the last time I had a shower, or shaved, and realized it had been well over two weeks. I also would love to have a change of clothes or at least be able to launder the ones I was wearing. They took us to our room which was an elaborate suite. We were both taken aback by the beauty of the room not to mention the spectacular view of the blue waters through the large glass doors that opened onto a beautiful balcony.

The suite consisted of a sitting area, a bedroom with two queen-sized beds, and a spacious bathroom which included a walk-in shower with a separate bathtub and complementary amenities. I was pleased to see soap, a razor, as well as toothpaste and toothbrushes.

The sitting area had a small refrigerator that contained cold beverages as well as a small microwave oven and a coffee pot with packets of coffee. There was also a large TV in the bedroom, and the bedspreads were made of beautiful blue satin. In the closet were two plush Terry Cloth robes with matching slippers. I had seen hotel rooms such as this on TV, but I certainly had never been in one.

I could tell by the excited look on Anis' face that she had never been in one either. For some reason, it popped into my head that this would be a perfect place to spend a honeymoon.

It was good to be back with Anis and to hold her close to me. I told her I had been so afraid that I might never see her again and I didn't think I could stand that. For the first time, I told her that I loved her. She said, "Oh Sonny, I love you too. I knew I felt something special between us the first time I saw you. Now I know that it was unconditional love that I have for you. I don't want to ever be without you in my life again."

We finally broke our embrace, and I made my way over to the sofa. It was very plush and comfortable. Before Anis joined me, she made a pot of coffee with the complimentary coffee that was provided. When the coffee was brewing, she came over and joined me on the sofa. The aroma of the coffee filled the air and smelled wonderful.

We talked about how we had misread Nadir and wondered what kind of plan they had for the rescue, and if it included the two of us, or just me. I told her that time would tell and that we would just have to wait and see. Soon, the coffee was ready, and Anis asked me how I liked mine. I told her there was only one way for a Scroggins to drink coffee – hot and black. Then she said, "I guess I will have to learn to drink it that way if I'm going to be a Scroggins, but for now, I like my cream and sugar."

She brought me a cup and then fixed hers. I was stunned by what she said about becoming a Scroggins, but I didn't make any comments on her statement. However, I knew that was what I wanted, but I must finish my mission before I could think seriously about anything else.

After drinking our coffee, she decided to go take her shower. Since they didn't have electricity on the island where she lived, she could only take a bath in a tub with water that was drawn from their well. She had no clothes other than the ones she was wearing. Neither did I. I told her she could wear one of the robes the hotel provided and could wash her clothes in the bathtub and use the hairdryer that was in the room to dry them. She thought that was a great idea and I said I would do the same with mine. I assured her that when she was wearing the robe that I would be a perfect gentleman and respect her modesty, to which she said, "Maybe I don't want you to."

That caught me off guard, and I told her to go take her shower. She was walking toward the shower and looked back over her shoulder and said with a smile, "Would you like to join me?" How tempting that invitation was, but I mustered up enough strength to resist and say, "When the time is right, but this is not the time."

While she was gone, I turned on the television and watched CNN News. There was a large fire burning out of control in northern California. I was surprised that would make the news in this part of the world, but so much of what happens in the United States affects the economy in this part of the world.

After a while, I heard the shower stop running, and then I soon heard the hairdryer blowing. I assumed that she had washed her clothes as I suggested. Later, she came out with her clothes back on, although they were still damp. But the thing that I liked about her was her long-wet hair. She said she needed to go back into the bathroom and dry her hair, but I told her I liked the way it looked and that I needed to go take my shower. I told her she was beautiful and that one day, we would have an intimate relationship. "I may be old-fashioned, but I still have the value that intimacy should wait until after you are married and that marriage is a lifetime commitment. So Anis, what I'm saying is that I want you to be my wife. I'm asking, will you marry me?"

Immediately, without any hesitation, she said YES, and in the same breath, she asked when we could be married. I wasn't ready for that either, so I impulsively said, "Right now."

"Now?" she asked.

"Sure, why not now? We should be able to find a preacher, priest, or someone that can marry us." I showered quickly and we left the hotel in quest of someone to perform a marriage ceremony. Since she had a somewhat Muslim faith, and since we were in their country, I suggested we have a Muslim ceremony and later we could have a traditional wedding in my country. "You mean in East Texas?" She asked.

"That's exactly what I mean," I said.

We found a mosque and asked the Qazi, also known as a Qadi, to marry us, but he refused because I was an unbeliever in the Muslim faith not to mention we had not complied with the three-day celebration requirement which was a feast for both the families of the bride and groom.

Next, we looked for a Catholic church in hopes we could find a priest that would marry us. After much searching, we found a cathedral, but the priest also refused to marry us because neither of us was Catholic. I asked Anis about local Yemen marriages, and she assured me that we could not get married because of Yemen customs. Boys and girls are not allowed to intermingle, and all marriages are arranged by their parents. Once the wedding is over, the newly married couple is expected to move in with the groom's parents and the bride is to serve her in-laws.

"Where is a justice of the peace when you need one?" I asked. She didn't even know what that was, and after I explained, she said she was sorry but there was no equivalent in this country. Then I had the idea of asking Armand to marry us! We could commit our lives to one another and exchange wedding vows before him and Nadir as our witnesses. Later when we get to east Texas, we can have a formal marriage ceremony. Anis was in agreement with that, so back to the hotel, we went to.

When we approached Armand with this idea, he thought we were crazy and questioned his credentials in a matter such as this. I told him that I would write a pledge that we would make to one another, and all he needed to do was sign as a witness that we indeed made those promises to one another. Finally, he agreed.

We went back to our room and I wrote, "*I, Sonny Scroggins, take you, Anis, to be my wedded wife; to have and to hold, from this day forward; for better, for worse; for richer, for poorer; in sickness and in health; to love and to cherish until we are separated by death; as God as my witness, I give you my promise."* Then I wrote similar vows for Anis and asked her if that sounded alright to her, and it did.

We stepped across the hallway and asked both Nadir and Armand to witness our exchanging wedding vows with one another. We held hands, and as we looked into each other's eyes, I promised my commitment to Anis and likewise she to me. Then we sealed our vows with a kiss while Nadir and Armand applauded.

Once that was finished, I asked Armand and Nadir to sign on the bottom of the page that they had witnessed our vows, which they did. After they extended their congratulations, I told the two of them that we would see them in the morning, but for now, we had other things to do. Anis laughed and said she was probably the only bride who got married with wet hair and wearing wet clothes.

When we got back to our room, I told Anis that it was our American custom for the groom to carry the bride over the threshold on their wedding night, so after opening the door, I picked her up in my arms and said, "Mrs. Scroggins, welcome to my world" as I walked through the doorway kicking it closed behind me.

The next morning, we got back to the business at hand. Anis and I went to Nadir's room. When we got there, he said there was a helicopter on a ship at the docks along with navigation and topographical maps of the Grand Canyon area. I told him we had tried to hike into that area, but it was too rugged. He agreed that it would be extremely difficult to hike very far into the canyon.

Then he showed me on a map a relatively flat spot about a mile north and over a hill from the chemical facility. He said he thought it would be level and open enough to land a helicopter plus the hill would provide cover as well as a sound barrier. He said I would need to fly very low to the ground and do it at night in order to avoid being detected. I told him it would be quite risky to fly that low in the dark in unfamiliar territory. He agreed but said there was no other way. "Not only that, you will also need to have all the lights on your chopper turned off," he added.

"Once you've landed, the helicopter will be your base station. You should be able to call us in case of an emergency on a special channel that is encrypted. After you land, you are to hike to a lake on your side of the facility. All your scuba gear will be on the helicopter. He showed me an aerial photo of where it was and said this was the water supply that was used in their chemical development.

It is here that you will dive and make your entrance into the plant. This also should be done under the cover of darkness. Once you get inside, it will be up to you to find your friends because we don't know where they are within the facility, but we know from our intelligence that they are on the inside and are being forced to work on a chemical countermeasure. This is why it is so crucial that we get them out of there to protect the design of our government's state-of-the-art warfare.

"Once I find them, how will I get them out?" For the first time, I saw Armand smile as he said, "Improvise." I knew that meant they didn't have a plan, but they did say that when we were airborne in the helicopter after the rescue, an aircraft carrier would be in the Red Sea waiting to pick us up and take us back home. Home. How wonderful that word sounded to my ears!

"What about my new bride?" I said.

"You will be able to fly her home before flying to the facility."

"Could she go along and help me? Once I get inside, it will be obvious that I am not part of them because of my size and skin color, but Anis could disguise herself as one of them and might be able to find Ron and Tim from the inside."

"Mr. Scroggins, we will let you make that call. You know the danger if she is involved, but that is your decision to make and not ours. We want you two to go back to your room and think about all that we have said, and we'll talk again in the morning."

When we got back to our room, I asked Anis if she felt we could trust Nadir and Armand. She said she did. "Otherwise, why would they have gone to the trouble of tracking you down and furnishing you with all the equipment that you need?" Then I asked her if she wanted to be a part of the team, or if she would rather I take her to her parents' home and wait for me there. She immediately said she wanted to go with me. I was glad to hear that although it might slow the logistics of the rescue a little bit. But, it would be well worth it to have her with me in spite of the risk. I loved her so much.

We sat down and came up with our plan and presented it to Nadir the next morning. I wanted to do a couple of "flyovers" just to become familiar with the terrain. Then we wanted to go by Anis' parents to tell them about our marriage and that she would be going with me to the United States. I would tell them that I would bring her back every few months for a visit. She would also need to pack her clothes and the things she wanted to take with her to America. I would also need a day or two to give Anis a quick course in deep-sea diving. After that we should be ready to go.

"You will be ready in seven days?" Nadir asked. I told him that I should be if I could get the helicopter today. He made a telephone call and said that it would be landing at the airport in about four hours. I was amazed at the contacts and the power he seemed to have in this country and the fact that he had to do everything "undercover".

"There is one more thing, Mr. Scroggins, that you need to understand very clearly. Should you get caught, we know nothing of this mission and none of our arrangements will be available to you. In other words, you will be on your own. Is that clear?"

"Yes, sir. I fully understand, and if that should occur, I will need to improvise," I said as I winked at Armand.

Anis and I went to the hotel restaurant for a bite to eat while we waited for the helicopter. After a while, a messenger came to our table and said, "Sir, will you and the lady come with me?" We followed him to a different car than Nadir had been in, but the driver took us to the airport and dropped us off on the tarmac where the helicopter was parked. Anis and I got out of the car and the driver drove away.

I gave the helicopter a quick visual inspection and noticed that the back-cargo area was packed with scuba equipment. I finally climbed into the pilot seat while Anis sat on the copilot side. Soon, the engines were running, and I turned to her and said, "Well, this is it. Are you ready?"

CHAPTER 14

After re-familiarizing myself with the R44, we received clearance to take off. I asked Anis to act as a liaison between the control tower and me, and we were soon in the air. Before long, we were flying over their Grand Canyon, and indeed the mountains appeared to be steep and rough. However, we already knew that from trying to hike up there. Then we flew near the chemical site. I maintained a high altitude and stayed a safe distance to the east so as not to draw suspicion.

I also spotted the clearing where Nadir wanted me to land. Once we cleared the facility, I looped back at a lower altitude. With the mountains as a shield, I flew over the landing spot. It looked to be safe enough from five hundred feet in the air. Then I pulled out and headed for the home of Anis' parents.

It took a little less than an hour to get there, and Anis had to show me which island was theirs. Soon, we were on the ground not far from their house. The entire family heard us as we approached, and when Anis and I got out of the helicopter, they couldn't believe what they were seeing! Quickly, they rushed over to us and hugged her with tears trickling down their cheeks.

Right away, we went into their house and Anis shared with them all of our news which included our marriage and plans to go to Texas, but she didn't tell them about our mission. Of course, I didn't understand a word she said, but I watched their body language, and I could sense their hurt and felt they had resentment toward me. Frankly, I certainly could understand their feelings. They seemed stunned to hear about our marriage. The more she talked, the warmer they seemed to be, and before she had finished, her father stood up, walked over to me, and extended his hand to me which I graciously accepted.

As I stood to accept his hand, he embraced me and kissed me on each cheek. I didn't know what she had told them about me, but apparently, it was enough to calm their fears. Then her dad left the house. Later, Anis told me she explained to them that I made her happy and that she would never find anyone that she could love as much as she loved me. Finally, they agreed that they wanted her to be happy and was good with our marriage, but they still were not too keen on her going with me to America.

Later, I went to the helicopter to check out what was inside the cargo area. There were two sets of scuba equipment, two wristwatches with a note explaining how to use them as a camera, binoculars, rope, bolt cutters, a camouflage net, a pistol with two boxes of bullets, a box of explosives, several packages of pressure-dried food, packages of instant coffee, and two changes of clothes for each of us in sealed plastics bags.

There was also a set of clothes for each of the two prisoners along with a windbreaker and a heavy coat. Wow! They seemed to have thought of everything! I was also glad to have a change of clothes as I had worn the same ones since the attack on the ship. I hoped mine would fit me, and they looked as though they would.

Later that afternoon, I took Anis to the beach for our first diving lesson. I knew I didn't have enough time to properly teach her to use her own equipment, so I planned to teach her to swim tandem with me on the buddy system. She would have her own mask, and we would swim side by side and share one air source. I would breathe and then give her the mouthpiece for a breath. We would alternate that method until we got to where we were going.

Once we were in the water, she was a little nervous and tense, but I told her to relax because I wasn't going to let anything happen to her. She relaxed and quickly got the hang of what I wanted her to do. She was a good swimmer and wasn't afraid of the water. We swam for a while until she felt comfortable with the buddy system.

That night, we shared the guest house together. I knew this was very awkward for Anis and her parents, but it was one of those things that would get easier with time. While we lay together with her head resting on my shoulder, we talked about the upcoming mission. I emphasized to her again how important the success of the mission was and how high the risk was. I said to her that in many ways, I wanted her to stay with her folks so she would be safe and let me go it alone. But on the other hand, I wanted her with me and thought she would be able to contribute in a way that I could not.

She sat up and said, "No, sir! I'm not staying here! You are my husband, and I plan to go and stay with you through thin or thick or for better or worse. You can count me in!" I loved her more than I thought it possible to love anyone and teased her for getting the "thick or thin" backwards.

Then she said, "Can you tell me why this rescue is so very important?" I told her that Ron and Tim were lead scientists on a classified program and had worked at a chemical plant in Ft. Worth. The Oman government had hired them to develop a chemical for them to use against Yemen. Apparently, Yemen found out about it through some kind of intelligence work and took Ron and Tim. They first kidnapped Tim, and Ron came to me to ask for my help in locating him. Soon afterward, Ron also disappeared, and I began to receive anonymous phone calls giving me clues. From the surveillance work that has been done, it seems that they were brought to this chemical facility and are being forced to develop a counter chemical that will make the Omen chemical ineffective.

"Why didn't they just kill them?" she asked in her cute Arabic voice.

"I don't know. Maybe they did. This rescue is simply based on a hunch and on some phone calls that I received. If they are still alive, my guess is that they didn't want to stop the production of the chemical, but rather they wanted an antidote to it. Perhaps, the development was too far along to simply stop it, and if those two were killed, others could carry on with the plans. So far, as we know and that we believe, they are not dead but are working in the facility we saw yesterday from the helicopter."

Then Anis asked, "Will the government of Oman pay you a lot of money if you rescue Tim and Ron?" I told her money had never been mentioned and I had no idea if they would or not. I was simply doing it to help a friend that I thought was in trouble. She said she was amazed that anyone would put their own lives in danger merely to help someone else and that was one of the many things she loved about me.

Then she said, "Well, I look forward to getting them out. Any ideas how?" I told her that I had none and wouldn't have until after we scoped out the place. Jokingly, I said I thought we could just walk in the front door and ask for their release and then leave with 'em.

Just before dark the next day, we gathered a good bit of food and water from Anis' mother along with the personal things that Anis wanted to take to America. Then it was time for us to leave. Anis spent a few minutes alone with her parents.

Finally, she made her way to the helicopter with tears flowing down her cheeks. I revved up the engine, she waved goodbye, and then we lifted off. After circling her home place once, we headed for the rugged mountains of Yemen. We should arrive there somewhere near midnight. Anis didn't say much during the flight, and I knew it was emotionally hard for her to leave her home and family so suddenly.

As we neared the landing site, I lowered the chopper to just a few hundred feet above the ground and turned off all the lights, including the one in the cockpit. I could see the instrument panel by occasionally using a flashlight. I felt that the small light could not be seen from the ground. In reality, I was flying mostly by engine sound and feel. Fortunately, there was a good bit of moonlight which helped me see the ground below. I carefully and slowly eased the chopper into place and then gently lowered it down until we were safely on the ground. Once I felt we were secure, I killed the engine.

"So far so good," I said to Anis. She complimented me on doing a masterful job of bringing the helicopter down and landing it. Then she asked, "Is there anything you can't do well?" I smiled and said there were plenty of things I could not do, much less do well.

Until daylight, we stayed inside the helicopter. With the engines off, it soon became cold, so we covered ourselves with blankets and tried to get some sleep while sitting in the cockpit seats.

I woke up when it was getting daylight, and while pulling the camouflage net from the cargo hold, I woke up Anis. She asked what I was doing, and I told her that we needed to cover the helicopter to avoid detection from any aircraft that might fly by. She hopped down and helped me, and with the two of us working together, it didn't take long to have it covered.

When that was completed, we hiked into the wooded area, and like before, we found some large rocks that would protect us on three sides, and we could build a campfire. These rocks formed a crevice like a small cave which protected us from the top as well as the sides. Soon, we had a cup of instant coffee, which wasn't the best in the world, but considering the circumstances, it was pretty good.

Before we finished our coffee, three helicopters flew over and appeared to land at the facility. I was so glad that we had covered our chopper with the net. This got my curiosity going, so we put out our fire and we each grabbed binoculars and started toward the facility. The hike was pretty rugged, but nothing to compare with what we had done a few days ago. After a short time, we made it to the crest of the hill that separated us from the facility, and then for the first time, I had a good view of the facility.

It was a rather large single-story building that was surrounded by a high-security fence. It was apparent that there were no roads in or out, but I did see a helipad. I figured the helicopters we saw a few minutes earlier were bringing in supplies and/or employees or both. I wondered if they came in every day, and I wondered, too, about the feasibility of me landing there for a quick get-a-way.

I didn't see any people on the outside of the facility, nor did I see any windows in the building, which might be a plus for us. Anis was surprised that there were no windows, but I told her most buildings where classified work was being done didn't have windows. They didn't want anyone to be able to look in and see what they were doing.

We stayed a safe distance away to avoid detection, but I did see security cameras all around the building and along the fence. While no one was in the yard, it was apparent that the outside was being watched through the cameras.

Anis and I worked our way around the mountain until we could see where the water intake from the lake was. There were large pipes going into the building from the lake. I'd guess the pipes to be at least three feet in diameter, maybe four. One was probably the intake while the other was the discharge. They had several bends and turns which would rule out anyone entering the plant through the pipes. As I studied this section, it looked like the fencing was vulnerable around the pipes. In fact, it looked like a person might be able to slip between the fence and pipe without cutting the wire.

I also noticed a door going into the building near where the pipes entered, and there were security cameras on each corner of the building pointed toward the pipes. However, it appeared that a person could crawl between the two pipes and use them as a screen to block themselves from camera detection. If anyone could get into the building itself, I doubt they would be detected by a camera as there would be no need to have them inside.

I told Anis that I thought I could get to the door with no problem, but from there, I had no idea what would happen. I really needed to get inside to see if I could locate Tim and Ron. I wondered if there were some kind of living quarters inside. I doubted that they allowed Tim and Ron to leave every night. I studied the roof for locations of vent pipes.

The bathrooms would need a vent pipe, and most of them were on the end where the pipes came in, which I hoped was good for us. I wondered if people worked throughout the night, or if the only people inside were the ones who were guarding Tim and Ron. And then I wondered if Tim and Ron were actually in there! Maybe this entire trip had been a wild goose chase, but if they were inside, they really didn't need to be guarded because where could they go? There was no feasible way in or out of this place other than by helicopter.

As we watched, a man came out the end door and monitored some gauges and adjusted one of the pipe valves before going back inside. He was wearing a white lab coat with an identification badge. If we could get a lab coat and a badge, maybe Anis could make her way inside and snoop around some.

We moved from the end of the building to where we could get a better view of the helipad and front entrance, which was all still enclosed by the perimeter fence. The front of the building had a large glass window with what appeared to be a security table just inside the door. My guess was that only authorized personnel were allowed beyond that security point. Anis said she was surprised to see a window since there were none on the back or the sides of the building.

While we were watching, I heard some choppers approaching. We took shelter and watched. There were two of them, and after they landed, eight people got off and entered the building--six men and two women. They were dressed in street clothes without lab coats. If they are workers, they apparently put the coats on when they get inside. By using our binoculars, we could tell that they were not wearing badges.

They stopped at the front desk, and soon they were met by someone and escorted farther into the building. While they were inside, the helicopters remained on the helipad with the pilots inside. I noticed that the choppers did not have any special markings, such as a company name or government logo, so maybe I could fly mine in without arousing any suspicions.

How could we get inside? I assumed the back door would be locked and would probably have an alarm that sounded when it is opened. After watching for a while, we saw six of the eight people return to the helicopters and fly away.

We went back to camp for a bite of lunch and to discuss our plans, as if we had any. I wondered if maybe we could go right through the front door with our rescue mission. If somehow we could get Ron and Tim to the front desk, they could make a dash to the helicopter, and we could be up and away. I told Anis that seemed easier than trying to rescue them by going under water.

We discussed what we could do and agreed that I needed to position myself near the backdoor and overpower the man that checks the meter, get his lab coat, and then have Anis wear it and go into the building. I described Ron to her, but I didn't know Tim. However, I figured Americans should not be too hard for her to spot. Before making our move, we watched the backdoor some more. It seemed that every three hours someone read the meter and adjusted the water flow. I couldn't figure out why, but that seemed to be the pattern. I wondered if it continued throughout the night.

While we watched, three helicopters arrived about five o'clock and hauled a crew of employees away. "This must be a daily commute," I told Anis. I wondered how many workers remained in the building at night. The sun was about to set, and it would soon be cold, so we headed back to camp for some warmer clothing before returning for our stakeout. If my theory was correct, someone would come out about eight o'clock and make an adjustment to the water inlet. Sure enough, just like clockwork, a man showed up and did his thing. Since it was well after dark, I decided that later tonight we would make our move.

All the security cameras around the perimeter fence that we noticed earlier in the day appeared to be directed toward the interior of the fence and not to the outside. If this was right, we might be able to ease up to the fence under the cover of darkness and not be detected. At least it was worth a try. So, the plan was to take a bag of dry clothes and then slip to the fence and toss the bag over the fence. Then Anis and I would ease into the water and work our way between the two large pipes and through the fence.

I felt we could crawl up to the building, and I hoped we would be out of the camera's viewing area. When the man came out to read the meter, I would club him from behind, tie and gag him, toss him between the pipes, and drag him outside the fence and stake him out in the water. While I was doing that, Anis would take his lab coat and walk over and pick up her bag of clothes. She would then hopefully get out of the camera's view and change into dry clothes, put the lab coat on, and walk into the building. Once inside, she would try to locate Ron and Tim, tell them who she was, and that I would soon be coming for them-- so they needed to be ready to move.

We didn't know if this would work or not, but there was only one way to know for sure, and that was to give it a shot. I gathered from the chopper some rope, bolt cutters, and a sharp knife while Anis put together a change of clothes in a plastic bag. I calculated that the man should be coming out about eleven, so about nine-thirty we headed that way.

We carefully made our way to the fence outside the back door, and I tossed Anis' bag over into the yard not far from the water lines. Then we retreated away into the darkness and watched. Nothing happened, so after what I thought was a safe amount of time, we eased into the water and swam to the water lines. We both dove into the water and surfaced between the pipes.

I'd guess there were about four feet of distance between the two pipes. I pulled Anis close to me as I worded a prayer asking for safety and success, kissed her, and then said, "Let's go."

We swam to the fence, but it was a little tighter around the pipes than I had thought. I used the bolt cutters to cut away a small part of the fence, and after a few minutes, we squeezed underneath the wire and swam to the water's edge where we crawled on our bellies to where the pipes went into the building. We lay motionless until I heard some movement inside the door. It opened to the outside, so I positioned myself to where I would be behind the door. As soon as the man came outside, I clubbed him with a short piece of pipe that I had picked up, and it appeared I knocked him out cold. We quickly closed the door and stripped him of his lab coat and badge. Anis put on the lab coat and picked up her dry clothes and tossed the wet ones back over the fence.

Meanwhile, I tied the man with the rope and dragged him outside the fence and into the water where I tied his hands to the discharge pipe. The water was well over his head, so the rope was all that kept him above the water. When Anis picked up her clothes, she used my clubbing pipe to push the nearby camera upward so that it was not focused directly on the water pipes.

Then I eased back to the building to where Anis was, and when I got there, she opened the back door and walked inside. I waited for an alarm to sound, but I didn't hear anything. I planned to remain by the door, and if it looked safe inside, she was to come back and get me. Otherwise, she would spy around on her own.

I stood by the door and waited. While I stood there, I heard someone coming toward me from around the outside corner of the building.

CHAPTER 15

I wasn't sure what to do as I could tell the intruders were getting closer and closer. I fell to the ground and snuggled up as close as I could against the water pipe in hopes that I might not be detected.

Soon, two men with flashlights rounded the corner and cast their lights up toward the camera. They were talking, and even though I couldn't understand what they were saying, I assumed they were talking about the camera and how it could have been moved from where it had been focused. Finally, one of them started talking on his two-way radio and maneuvered the camera around with a stick that he had brought with him that had a hook on the end. He would push a bit and then talk on the radio, push and talk, and push and talk. Finally, he stopped. I assumed he had the camera adjusted where the person inside could see the area he wanted to see. I figured we would have been detected if Anis had not tilted the camera. I hoped they would leave and go back the way they came, but not so.

I feared they were going to check the camera on the other corner of the building, which meant they would come right by me. Fortunately, I had the darkness in my favor, but as they climbed over the pipe where I was lying, one of them spotted me. Immediately, both flashlights were shinning in my face! I leaped up, and with the pipe in my hand, I landed a hard blow to one of their heads, but the other one put up a struggle. Because of my larger size, I was able to get a chokehold on him, and he soon passed out, but I released him before he died.

With both of them lying on the ground unconscious, I had to make a quick decision as to what to do. I couldn't leave because Anis was inside. I couldn't stay because the ones on the inside would soon miss these two and come looking for them. I could tie them up with the man I had left in the water, but that would still lead to more of an investigation. I wondered why no one had come to look for the man who was reading the gauges. Apparently, they hadn't realized he was missing.

Finally, I decided to go inside the building. I hoped that when these two men were discovered, they would assume that I was outside and had fled, especially if I locked the door behind me which would indicate that I could not have entered the building.

So, I quickly opened the door and darted inside and pulled it closed behind me. Once inside, I looked for someplace to hide, but all I saw was a long empty hallway with a few crossing halls and doors up and down the corridor. I did see a small switch with a small light near the end door, which I assumed to be the alarm. I locked the door and flipped the switch to the "on" position and the light illuminated green.

I noticed some restrooms not too far up the hall, and I darted into the women. I hid out in one of the stalls in hopes that Anis might come in. I waited and waited, but no one came in at all. I glanced at my watch, and it was one-fifteen in the morning. This might help explain why the halls were so empty, but I was very concerned about where Anis might be.

Not knowing what to do or where Anis was, I sat in the stall for almost an hour before someone came in. She went into the stall next to where I was hiding, and I could tell by looking at the shoes beneath the partition separating the stalls that it was Anis!

"Anis?" I whispered.

"Sonny, is that you?" was the immediate reply.

"Yes, come over here."

She came to where I was, and we closed the stall door before I explained to her what had happened. I asked if she found Tim and Ron, and she said she did. They were, as I expected, in a small living quarter toward the back corner of the building. I asked her if we could go get them right now, but she thought not. She said the room was locked with a cipher code plus there were two guards outside their door and one staying inside the room.

"How did you get inside?" I asked. She said she found the janitorial room and grabbed a mop bucket and mop. Then she knocked on the door and asked the guard to let her in as she was instructed to clean the floor and had her hands full, and he did. Since she was wearing the lab coat and badge, they didn't pay much attention to her.

Then she said, "I could tell by the size of the men on the bunks that they were Americans. I recognized Ron from the description you gave me, and I made my way to where he was sleeping and nudged him enough to wake him. I instructed him to listen and not to open his eyes. While he pretended to be asleep, I quietly told him who I was and that you and I were going to get him and Tim out of here and that they needed to be ready. Then, I asked him where the lab they worked in was located. He whispered without ever opening his eyes that it was toward the front of the building — the first door on the right past the security desk. Then I mopped on past him. The guard was in the corner reading a book and wasn't paying any attention to me. When I finished mopping the room, I left, and here I am now."

"Great work!" I told her as I pulled her close for a big hug. "Where is the janitor's closet?" I asked. She told me that it was just a few feet from the lab and across the hall. I told her we needed to get out of here and back to camp because we needed to plan what to do next, plus I was getting cold in these damp clothes.

She eased out into the hall and motioned to me that all was clear, so I slipped out of my hiding place and to the door of the women's restroom. I watched as Anis rolled the mop bucket to the janitor's room before returning to me. Then she made her way down the hall to the end door and motioned to me that all was clear.

I hurried to catch up with her and looked out the peep hole in the door and saw that the place was swarming with people who I presumed were looking for me. There was no way we could get out just yet. So, we rushed back to the janitor's room where I hid while Anis stood in the hall nearby with her mop and bucket pretending to be mopping the hallway.

She worked her way up to the security desk where there was only one officer on duty, and he too was reading a magazine, but she noticed that all the security monitors were underneath the desk and she noticed also that several men were searching all around the build-ing. She spent a lot of time mopping the lobby so she could look at the monitors. Finally, things slowed down, and it looked to her as if the coast was clear. She came back to me, and again we headed for the back door, but before we did, I put on a lab coat and cap that I found inside the janitor's room.

Just before we got to the door, a guard came from one of the side rooms and saw us. As we heard the door opening, Anis quickly handed me the mop, and I kept my back to him as I was mopping the floor. Anis turned to him and said something in Arabic, which she later told me was, "Be careful as the floor might be slick."

Once this man was in the restroom, I looked outside and didn't see anyone. I turned off the door alarm and quickly went outside. Anis rushed the mop bucket back to the closet and soon met me outside. Like before, we crawled back to the water between the pipes, through the fence, and to the prisoner. I untied him from the pipe and took him with us. Anis grabbed her bag of clothes, and the three of us headed into the darkness toward the chopper. It was beginning to be daylight when we got back to camp.

I soon had a fire going, and we each huddled close to it to warm and to dry. Anis tried to talk to the man we had captured, but he refused to talk. After we warmed a bit, we heated up some freeze-dried food for breakfast. While the man didn't talk, he did eat as Anis put the food into his hands.

After eating and drying a bit, the sun was up, and the helicopters flew over us again and landed at the facility. Anis tried to get our prisoner to tell us what was going on, but like a good soldier, he said nothing. Since he wouldn't talk, I told Anis what I had in mind.

I said that late tonight, like last night, we would again slip up to the facility and position explosives underneath the discharge pipe. After that, we would also place some along the outer wall of the facility. If the building door was unlocked, I wanted her to go back inside and place some explosive patches behind things like a water fountain or fire extinguishers.

I told her that once the explosives were in place, we would return to camp and to the helicopter and the next morning fly and land it in front of the building. She would wear her lab coat and walk inside to the security table. Once she is inside, from the helicopter, I would remotely detonate the explosives, beginning with the water pipe. When the pipe ruptures, the entire courtyard should flood with water. After that, I would blow out the walls in the back of the building and follow with the interior walls. That should be enough of a diversion at the back of the building to allow us to storm the lab, grab our men, rush to the helicopter, and be gone.

Anis was a little apprehensive but thought it might work. She was afraid that with all the explosions, someone would get hurt or killed. I agreed, but I explained that the most powerful explosion patch would be outside on the water pipe. The other ones would not be very powerful. What I wanted was a lot of noise and chaos to allow us to storm the lab without being detected.

"What if we get caught?" she asked.

"I hate to guess what might happen, especially after we blow up their place. We just don't need to get caught!" I replied.

I then asked her if she knew how to use a pistol, and she said, "Not really." I got the pistol out of the cargo hull, and without the clip inserted, I showed her how to use it. I explained about the safety button and showed her how to aim. I told her that this gun was semiautomatic which meant that every time she pulled the trigger, it would fire as long as there were bullets in the clip. Then I showed her how to insert a new clip. For the next little while, she spent her time messing with the pistol until she felt pretty comfortable with it.

The rest of the day we lay around napping a little and waiting for dark. We made sure the prisoner was securely tied, and we also shared our food with him. I was still surprised that no one was out looking for him. Perhaps, he had asked to take off a few days or had a vacation scheduled. Thinking about that made us wonder if he had a wife and family who were worried because he didn't come home. Even though I considered him to be an enemy, I still had compassion for him. He was probably only an employee at the facility who was trying to make a living for his family and knew nothing about the chemical aspect of it. Still, I needed to stop thinking along those lines and focus on the mission that lay ahead of us!

Anis and I talked about a lot of things that happened to us while we were kids. Our backgrounds were very different. Mine was filled with love and support from family members. Hers was also filled with love, but it was not displayed. Most people in their culture did not show affection and feelings toward one another.

Throughout the day, she tried to talk with the prisoner but had little success. He finally thanked her for the food, but that was his limit. Finally, the day had passed, and after the evening helicopters had made their run, we uncovered the chopper and stowed the net back inside the cargo hull. As it approached midnight, we put a blanket over the prisoner, and Anis and I headed toward the facility with a bag of explosive material.

I explained to her that the explosive mass looked like modeling clay that you simply stick to a surface. After it was in place, a detonator was inserted that could be ignited by a remote signal. That's what I'd do from the helicopter. But our first order of business was to merely place the explosive patches.

Like before, she carried a bag of dry clothes in case she went inside, and like before, we used the pipes to slip up to the building without being detected. I carefully positioned an explosive patch underneath the discharge pipe and inserted a detonator. Then I hugged the building and made my way to each corner and stuck a patch beneath each camera mount. After that, we tried the end door, but it was locked. Rather than trying to force it open and run the risk of setting off the alarm, we stuck some explosive patches under the intake water pipe and grabbed our clothes bag and left.

Once we got back to the camp, we rebuilt the fire to warm and changed into some dry clothes. We settled down beside the fire in hopes of getting a little rest, but my adrenalin was so high that I could not get to sleep for thinking about what was going to happen soon. While I was running so many thoughts through my head, at least I felt more in control than when I was on the ship. I could have some influence on what happened here rather than simply being a victim. Armand told me to improvise and that was what I was doing.

As I thought about things, I began to wonder if the explosive igniter worked. I had never tried it and could not try it this close to the facility. I had to have enough faith in Nadir not to give me something that wouldn't work. So far, everything he provided functioned as I expected, so why should I doubt this would work?

I wanted to get to the facility before the morning choppers came with the employees. The fewer people who were there, the better our odds were. I told Anis that our plans had been altered a bit. I wanted her to dress in her lab coat and go to the guard station. "Convince him to let you in and then make your way to the back door and retrieve the explosive patches that we placed under the intake water pipe. After that, try to position them in strategic places inside the building. Once you have them placed and ready, come back to the front lobby with your mop bucket. That will be my signal to detonate."

Just a little past daylight, I fired up the helicopter and let it idle a few minutes before taking off. As it was warming up, I took a knife that was in the helicopter and stuck it in a tree somewhat near the prisoner. After we were gone, he could make his way there and cut himself free, but he would not have enough time to get to the facility to warn them.

Finally, after a prayer, a hug, and a kiss, I said to Anis, "Let's go."

We lifted off, and within minutes, I touched down on the helipad. Anis, wearing her lab coat, got out and entered the building. I sat in the helicopter with the engine idling. My hands were sweaty, and my heart was racing. I anxiously watched as she was trying to convince the guard to let her go inside. Finally, he gave her a badge, and she walked out of my sight.

I waited for what I thought was sufficient time for her to make it back to the lobby, but she had not shown. What should I do? Was she captured? Should I leave and return later, or should I crash the building with bullets blazing? Should I go on and blow the explosives that were already in place with the risk of hurting Anis, or should I wait? I felt something was dreadfully wrong.

CHAPTER 16

Finally, I decided that I couldn't leave Anis behind nor could I take the chance on having her injured by the explosions. I grabbed the pistol and tucked it into my trousers, put the detonator in my pocket, climbed out of the helicopter, and started toward the front door. Just before I got there, Anis showed up in the lobby behind the security guard.

The detonator had four buttons for sequence explosions. I stopped and took it out of my pocket and pressed button number one. I heard a tremendous explosion at the back of the building. Then I pressed button number two, and there was another explosion. By this time, all hands were rushing toward the back of the building or else taking cover. Then I pressed buttons 3 and 4 which ignited the explosives that Anis had just planted inside the building.

I stormed into the building and pistol-whipped the guard. Then Anis and I quickly made our way into the lab. As we entered the door, I saw Ron and a man I presumed to be Tim. When they saw me, I motioned for them to come with me, and they came running. We left the lab and were headed toward the front door when bullets began to buzz around us. The security guards took note of what was happening, and I told Anis to take Ron and Tim and get them aboard the chopper while I tried to slow down the guards.

I used the guard's desk as a blind and began firing back down the hall toward the approaching guards. I was glad that I had blown the discharge water line so the gushing water would keep any guards from coming around the back of the building on the outside.

I glanced and noticed Anis and the guys were in the helicopter, so I shot a few more rounds down the hall before making a dash for the chopper. By the time I got there and inside the cockpit, the guards were coming out of the building with bullets blazing all around us. This reminded me of my days in Viet Nam. I lifted off, and soon we were in the air and safely away from their gunfire.

I glanced back at Ron and said, "Hey, Buddy, how ya doing?"

"Much better," he replied with a smile and tears running down his cheeks. "I absolutely couldn't believe it when your lovely wife appeared in our room the other night and told me you were coming to rescue us. If I live to be a thousand years old, I can never repay you for what you have done for us."

Tim's voice was too quivery for him to talk much, but he put his hand on my shoulder and squeezed it and said, "Thank you. I never believed anything so wonderful could have happened to us." We didn't talk much more as both of them were very emotional.

After about ten minutes, I felt the chopper begin to vibrate. Immediately I realized that some of the gunshots had done some damage to the helicopter. I had felt similar vibrations in Viet Nam, and every time it was from gunshot damage. The oil pressure was dropping as well as the fuel.

Thankfully, the blades and tail rotor didn't seem to be damaged, which meant I still had some limited control, but I knew I had to put the chopper down. As I looked below, there was no good place to land. The mountains were rough with jagged peaks, not to mention being covered with trees. While I was looking, there was an explosion in the chopper, and the oil pressure dropped to zero. Smoke was billowing from the engine, and the control stick seemed to give me little control. I yelled out, "Brace yourselves! We're going down!"

I controlled the chopper the best I could as I tried to find the most level place for a crash landing. Soon we were clipping the treetops with the bottom of the chopper, and when the rotor blades hit them, we flipped and crashed through the trees and landed upside down.

Once all the dust settled, I checked on the others, and all three of them seemed to have survived the crash alright. Tim had a bruised knee and Ron had a cut above his right eye. I rushed over to Anis who was on the ground outside the aircraft. When I got there, she said she was alright, and I embraced her. When I let her go, I noticed blood on my shirt.

"Anis, you're hurt!" I cried out. She assured me that she was alright, but the more I quizzed her, she finally said that she took a bullet during our escape. Then she showed me her left side which had a huge hole right below the rib cage. Her shirt was soaked in blood. I knew we had to do something to stop the bleeding, or else she would bleed to death in these mountains.

I told Ron and Tim to drag out the camouflage net in the cargo hull and try to cover the helicopter the best they could. I figured the sky would soon be swarming with Yemen Air Force Pilots looking for us, and if they found us, they would finish us off.

While they were doing that, I looked for a place where I might be able to build a fire without being detected from the air. The terrain was very steep and full of rocks and crevices. I soon found what looked to be a shallow cave and quickly got Anis inside it. After a few minutes, I had a fire going and heated the blade of my knife in the fire.

I ripped her shirt off, and it looked like the bullet went all the way through her body which was a good thing. I told her that I needed to cauterize the wound to try to stop the bleeding. She, being a former medical student, knew exactly what I was talking about. I told her the only way I knew to do it was with a hot knife blade. She knew it would be extremely painful, and I wished like everything there was some other way. She understood. Soon, the knife blade was red hot, and I picked it up and looked at her with tears in my eyes. She said, "Let's go", as she gritted her teeth tightly. I pressed the knife against her side. She flinched and gritted her teeth more tightly. I could smell the flesh burning as I held the knife on the wound.

Before I removed the knife, her body went limp and lifeless. I cried out, "Oh no! Don't leave me now!" Then I noticed that she was still breathing, and I breathed a sigh of relief. Apparently, she had passed out from the shock of the pain, which was probably a good thing because I needed to cauterize the exit wound in her back also. I rolled her over, and after reheating my knife, I pressed it to her bare flesh. Again, the smell of burning flesh made me almost nauseous. Finally, it was over.

I hadn't noticed one, but almost all aircraft have a first-aid kit somewhere onboard. I pulled off my jacket and laid Anis on it while I went back to the chopper. Ron and Tim had just about completed covering the helicopter. Each of them thanked me again and again for all the trouble I had gone to for the rescue and they felt doubly bad that Anis was hurt. They were just as shocked as I was that she had gotten shot because she never let on in the slightest way. While they made their way to the cave, I dug around the helicopter, and sure enough, tucked up under the pilot's seat was a first-aid kit.

I took it and rushed back to where I had left Anis. She was still unconscious, and I was reluctant to wrap the wound for fear that the tender flesh around it might stick to the wrap. I placed some gauze on the wound before wrapping it. When I was at the chopper, I grabbed another shirt for Anis. While this was not the time for modesty, I knew she would feel better if she was covered, and her old shirt was now in rags.

I asked Ron if he would scout around for some water while Tim gathered some of the food rations from the cargo hull. Both men were more than willing to oblige while I sat by the side of my lovely bride. After a bit, she began to regain consciousness.

Naturally, the first thing she wanted to know was where she was and what had happened. As I began to explain, it all came back to her. I told her that she took a bullet and that I cauterized the wounds to stop excessive bleeding, which seemed to have worked. She looked up at me with her dark brown eyes and said, "That's good, but what about infection?"

I told her I was concerned about that also and hopefully, we could get her out of these mountains quickly and to a hospital for treatment.

By this time, Ron had returned and said he found a stream of water no more than a hundred yards down the mountain. He was glad to see Anis sitting up and talking. He said she had told him she was my wife the night she was whispering to him in his bed when she was pretending to be the cleaning lady. Otherwise, he wouldn't have believed she was anything other than a maid. While we were talking, Tim returned with some food, and he was also glad to see the improvement in Anis. He told me I was a lucky man to have her as a wife, and I told him I totally agreed with him.

Without her help, the rescue would not have been possible because I couldn't have pretended to be an employee nearly as effective as she did; for one thing, I couldn't speak their language.

After eating, we sat around the fire and talked. Ron and I had a lot to catch up on. I asked how he got those messages to me about the Grand Canyon. He said he never sent any messages. I said, "You mean you never called me saying that you were in the Grand Canyon?"

"No, honest in'jun. I never made any phone calls to anyone," Ron replied.

"Well, somebody did. Somebody wanted me to find and rescue you," I said, and all the while my mind locked in on Kali. "What do you know about Kali Huff?" I asked.

"Oh, not much," Ron said. "She is a good looker. I guess you met Kali?"

"Yeah, I met her, and I'm not too sure I trust her."

Tim spoke up and said that she came to work at ChemTec in a management position, which seemed a little strange, as it had always been company policy to promote from within. However, she seemed very qualified to do the job she assumed, so no one really complained or questioned.

Out of curiosity, I asked Ron how he knew when we first got together about the need for a person with both helicopter and scuba diving skills. "Did you know where Tim was?"

He said he had a good idea that Tim had been taken by the Yemen government because of a mysterious telephone call warning him to sabotage the chemical program if we ever hoped to see Tim alive again. "I didn't know where to go or what to do, so I confided in Kali, who I had been dating. I made light of her a few minutes ago, but we were really pretty close. She mentioned a remote facility in Yemen where they did a lot of secret research, and from what she said and the way she said it, I suspected she thought that might be where Tim was being held. I quizzed her on how she knew all that and she told me her brother mentioned it to her.

During our talk, she said the only way in or out of the facility was by helicopter. After that, I did a little digging and found the site on the map and discovered the supply lake for the facility and figured that might be another way inside for a scuba diver."

"So, you really formed your opinion based on what Kali said?" I replied.

"Yeah, that pretty much sums it up. After what she said, I connected the dots."

Then I asked him about being apprehended. He said it was a surprise attack in his apartment. Four men came in and overpowered him, forced him into a car, and then they drove to a private jet that was waiting at a small airstrip north of Ft. Worth. "From there, the rest is history."

Then I changed the subject by asking Tim, since he was a scientist if he knew any way to fight an infection if Anis got one from her open wound. He thought for a moment and then said, "I remember reading years ago about how the Indians used to fight what they called "the fever" by boiling water ferns, taking the sap, and mixing it with red clay to make a paste. Then they would cover the body with the paste, or if there was an open wound, they would pack the wound with it and then wrap it with either live oak leaves or cedar branches. They felt the evergreen foliage was symbolic of life. "From the reports I read, it seemed to work. You know there is a lot of sugar and energy bottled up in tree sap. Some people make syrup from the sap of maple trees."

I didn't know where we were, but I felt like it was going to be a couple of days before we could get back to civilization. What Tim said might work. I certainly didn't want Anis to come down with a bacterial infection way out here, or anywhere for that matter. Out here, it could kill her. I decided that in the morning I would ask Tim if he could find what he needed to make up the old Indian paste.

It was mid-afternoon, and if we had not had the misfortune, we would be on an aircraft by now getting ready to go back to America — but that certainly was not the case. We let Anis rest while Ron, Tim, and I spent the rest of the afternoon talking. Several times, we heard jet and helicopters flying overhead, but with the netting on the chopper, we were not detected.

Apparently, they didn't have any heat-sensing devices, but if they did, they should not be able to detect our body heat as long as we remained in the cave. This was another reason for laying low for a while.

It became dark and the night air had a chill in it. We built a good fire that heated the cave we were in and allowed for a good comfortable night's sleep.

The next morning, we were up early. It seemed that I always woke up early when I slept outdoors surrounded by nature. My thoughts flashed back to east Texas and the wonderful times I had when we camped out down on the creek. My thoughts came back to the present and I enjoyed hearing a host of birds singing, and as I looked through the trees, I saw several squirrels darting here and there. Ron soon had the fire blazing again and had gone after some water.

Anis said she was sore but thought she could walk. I wasn't so sure of that. I wanted to observe how well she moved around in the cave before we headed out over the rugged terrain that would require stretching and climbing and maybe even jumping. The last thing we wanted to happen was for her wounds to start bleeding again. Later I asked Tim if he thought he might be able to find what he needed to make that Indian paste. He scouted around but later returned empty-handed. "No such luck," he said as he shrugged his shoulders.

We decided to lay low for the rest of the day before trying to hike out. We had crashed near a mountainside not very far from the top rim of the mountain range. We didn't know if it would be best to stay near the top or try to go down toward the river. I told them that parts of the river were impassable.

As we talked, Tim spotted some people below us making their way through the woods. Immediately we all got quiet and hunkered down with our eyes peeled toward the timber below. Then I saw them! There were four Yemen soldiers, and each had a backpack and rifle. "This changes things," I whispered to Ron and Tim. "I'm not sure in what way, but it certainly changes things."

I knew we would have to be more careful as we traveled; I knew we probably couldn't build a fire, and I knew if they spotted us that we couldn't overpower them. I wasn't sure what to do, but things had certainly changed. Fortunately, they did not spot the helicopter because of the netting, but who is to say there won't be more coming, and it likely will just be a matter of time before they find us.

I was wondering why they were here. Did they know our chopper had crashed? We were far enough from the facility that they couldn't have seen us. I was low enough in altitude to not be detected by their radar. Were they in this dense, rugged place looking for us?

The only thing I could figure was that they did have heat-sensing devices and sensed the heat from the helicopter engine yesterday as they were flying over. Perhaps the engine heat from the helicopter had not cooled down enough to avoid detection. Then Ron spoke up and said, "Maybe those guys aren't looking for us at all; maybe they are on some kind of training mission."

I hadn't thought about that. I just figured they were looking for us, but my instincts were wrong about Nadir, and I guess they could be wrong again. However, that doesn't change the need for us to be vigilant and on our toes.

While we left Anis inside the cave for some R & R, Tim, Ron, and I went to the chopper to gather all that we thought we would need and could carry on our journey. We got the rope, binoculars, axe, and food. I wanted to take the compass from the cockpit but couldn't get it out. I did get the maps of the area, but the problem was I didn't know where we were to pinpoint on the map.

I could make a pretty good guess based on how long we flew before crashing and based on my estimate, I figured we were about ten miles away from any road. It was also apparent from looking at the map that the best route to take was the mountain tops and not the river.

The rest of the day was quiet, and we didn't have any more visitors.

The next morning, we loaded up what we could carry and started on our hike to safety. After we reached the mountain crest, the hiking was a bit easier as there were no major cliffs to scale, but this came at the cost of no water streams or caves for protection; however, we were still pretty well protected by the dense timber.

The going was slow as Tim was favoring his hurt knee and Anis was moving slowly because of her gunshot wound. So, every few minutes, we stopped to rest. So far, Anis's wounds were not bleeding and hopefully, they won't. She is just extremely sore and weak from her blood loss.

We hiked until a few hours before dark, and then we began searching for a good campsite. We found nothing as good as where we were at the crash site. There were no caves to be found and not very many large rocks. We were mostly in a thick, heavily wooded area. After discussing it, we decided we needed to build a fire in spite of the risk. We needed the warmth since the nights were cold, and we had no covering to sleep under.

My biggest fear was having the fire spotted from the air. Fortunately, we had not seen the soldiers again, and I assumed we wouldn't be threatened by them seeing the campfire. We all agreed that the need outweighed the risk.

None of us slept very well as we continually had to get up and stoke the fire with new wood, not to mention lying on the rough, cold ground. Early in the morning before daylight, I looked at Anis by the firelight and noticed her face looked flush. I touched her and she was burning hot with fever! My biggest fear was coming to pass. It appeared that her body had gotten an infection from the open wounds being exposed to the unsanitary environment of the wild.

I figured we had traveled about six miles, and with any kind of good luck, we should make it out of the mountains by tomorrow — but will she be able to hang on that long? I wanted to get up and leave right away, but I knew we couldn't travel in this wilderness in the dark. We had to wait until daylight. I wished I had some cool water to rub her body with hoping to bring the fever down, but no such luxury was available.

CHAPTER 17

I didn't even try to sleep the rest of the night. As soon as there was a crack of light, I got the others up, and we were on our way. The men recognized the urgency of getting Anis out of these mountains and to a hospital. About mid-morning, we came to a spot where the mountain literally dropped off several hundred feet straight down. There was no way we could begin to scale down that cliff even in the best of conditions and health. The only choice we had was to backtrack a ways and head down off the mountain top toward the river.

The walking was difficult, and Anis' fever persisted. One fortunate thing was that as we got farther down the mountainside, we came across a stream that gave us an opportunity to give her a cool bath. The bathing brought her fever down dramatically, but we all knew that it would soon come up again. But for the moment, she felt a little better. We continued to press onward and westward.

Finally, we reached the valley floor, and we could look back and see the massive cliff that had stopped us. Now we were beyond that, and I figured we were just a few more miles from reaching the mountain road that would lead us to the farmer's house where we stayed before.

As we made our way beside the river's edge, I suddenly heard a gunshot and felt the air of the bullet as it whizzed by my ear. I yelled for the others to keep going while I stayed behind to try to detain the intruders.

I crouched down behind a fallen log and watched. It wasn't long before I saw the four Yemen soldiers following behind Ron, Tim, and Anis. As they neared me, I took careful aim with my pistol and fired. My shot was accurate as one of the soldiers fell to the ground, and the other three took cover.

Using the trees as cover, I maneuvered myself to another position a little farther downriver. I imagined I was feeling a lot like the snipers did in Viet Nam. I found another good location to crouch and wait. After a little while, I saw the soldiers making their way toward me, but this time there were only three, and they were more cautious. I was well hidden, and as soon as they were within range, I scored another fatal blow.

This time, instead of retreating, the remaining two soldiers stood their ground and opened up their rifles in my direction. I ducked below the large log that I used as cover, and no bullet even came close to hitting me as the soldiers were simply shooting blindly in my general direction. Finally, they stopped shooting and said something to one another. Then they slowly started walking in my direction with their rifles up and pointing.

Being well-concealed, I took aim once more and then shot and downed another one. Now only one was left. Again, there was a barrage of fire in my direction, but this time the soldier was retreating as he fired.

I got up to make my move, and as I did, he saw me and opened fire again. This time, I was hit in my right shoulder and fell to the ground. The pain was excruciating, but I lay motionless as if I was dead, and I had the pistol in my hand ready to fire. As I lay there, I remembered the story my dad told about how he apprehended a guy named Carl Lee. As the lone soldier came near me, he used his foot to try to roll me over, and as he did, I shot him right between the eyes.

I got up and hoped that would be the end of this manhunt, but before I left, someone was trying to talk with him on his radio. We had to get out of here and quickly! I picked up the soldier's rifle and headed out to find the others.

The more I rushed to catch up with them, the weaker I became. Finally, I stopped and took some broad leaves from a nearby tree and packed the leaves into my bullet hole. I had the same problem that Anis did, which was excessive bleeding. I pressed the leaves into place and held them tightly with my other hand. It was getting dark, and I had not found my companions. I didn't know if they were still ahead of me or if I had unknowingly passed them, or if had they been apprehended. Should I keep going, or should I stop and wait?

I decided to keep going. If I got to the road without finding them, then I could stop and wait. I pressed onward, but I could tell that I was not going to be able to continue much longer. I eased down to the river and washed my face which revived me somewhat, but I was hurting and tired and hungry. Nevertheless, the longing to reunite with my true love kept me moving forward.

Finally, well into the night, I saw the glimmer of a fire. This must be them! I made my way toward the fire. But when I got closer, I saw that it was another band of soldiers. Now, what was I to do? Did they have my people captive, and if so, did they think Anis was one of them and were they taking care of her? I figured they would keep Ron and Tim alive because they were of some value to them, but they would kill me in a heartbeat and glory in it.

I wondered if it was one of them who was calling the last soldier that I shot. Things were beginning to get fuzzy to me. I felt like I was about to pass out, but I couldn't afford to at this time. Somehow, I mustered up enough strength to stay conscious. I didn't see my people, but that didn't mean they were not there. After watching for a few minutes, I determined that there were only four soldiers. I eased nearer to the campsite, and with the soldier's rifle, I shot all four of the men before they had time to respond.

When I went into their camp, I didn't find Ron, Tim or Anis. They were not there. But I did find some hot food, which I ate and enjoyed, and one of the soldiers had a first-aid kit in his backpack. I took it and doctored my wound the best I could, using my left hand. I made my way back to the river and continued moving down the river until I collapsed.

The next thing I knew, I was waking up inside a cellar. I didn't know where I was or how I got there. Where were the others? Where was Anis? I didn't know where I was, but I knew that I had to get out of here! As soon as I stood from the cot where I was lying, the door opened, and Ron and Tim rushed in and closed the door behind them. They motioned for me to be quiet, which I did.

I could hear some talking above us, but after a while the talking stopped, and the door opened again. To my amazement, in came the farmer who had befriended us before! Now I really had some questions.

Ron told me that they made their way out of the mountains, and Anis led them to the farmer's house. The farmer remembered her and took them in. She talked with him, and soon after, he hid all of them in this cellar. "Several times, soldiers have come here looking for us, but he has sent them away. The day after we arrived, the farmer went looking for you, and several hours later, he returned with you in the back of his pick-up. It was obvious that you were hurt, so he doctored you the best he could and then brought you down here."

"How about Anis? Where is she?"

Ron gave a big pause, and I knew something bad had happened. "The farmer took her into Aden to the hospital. When he returned, he shrugged his shoulders and shook his head. Since he doesn't understand English and we couldn't understand him, we don't know what he said, but he held his hands to his face like a child sleeping, so we inferred from that gesture that Anis didn't make it. Sonny, I'm so sorry."

I was stunned! Now it really didn't matter to me if I survived or not. My purpose for living was over. I would never be able to show her off to my family in east Texas. I feared this might happen, but now that I faced the harsh reality of losing her, I wasn't sure that I could deal with it.

After a long silence, Ron finally said the farmer patched up my wound but didn't dare take me to the hospital with all the people out looking for me.

We stayed hidden there for a few more days until I was able to travel and the manhunt had eased. Then the farmer drove us to the farmers market in Aden. What a wonderful man he had turned out to be and we couldn't even talk to each other! From the market, we walked to the Mercure Hotel. All of this was filled with memories of Anis and me being there together. I told the guys that this is where we were married. Once we were in the lobby, I took the emergency phone number that Nadir had given to me and dialed it. Someone answered in Arabic. I said, "Nadir", and it wasn't long before Nadir was on the phone.

All I said was, "This is Scroggins. I am at the Mercure Hotel and we need to meet." After I hung up, we sat in the lobby and waited. This time there were three of us Americans waiting which caught the attention of some. After about thirty minutes, a man walked up to me and said, "Mr. Scroggins, you and your friends come with me." We got up and followed him into the elevator and up to the seventh floor. I soon realized that we were going to the same room we went to before.

We went inside, and Nadir was standing by the window with his back to us looking out over the courtyard. When he heard us, he turned, and I introduced him to Ron and Tim. He asked about Anis, and I told him that she didn't make it and neither did his helicopter. "But here are you scientists! Obviously, we missed our ride, so how do we get back to our country?" I asked.

Nadir said for us to stay here in the hotel lobby until he could make some arrangements. He commended me on a job well done and expressed his regrets over the loss of Anis. Then he wished us a good day and turned his back on us again. We knew that was our cue to leave the room.

We didn't have to wait very long in the lobby before one of Nadir's drivers came and got us and took us to the airport. There we boarded a helicopter where we were flown to a US Aircraft Carrier that was out in the Indian Ocean. What a wonderful feeling to be back among Americans that spoke English! Immediately, they took us to the medical clinic where the doctors gave us a physical exam and dressed my wound. They also started me on some antibiotics.

After our physical exam, we retired to our sleeping quarters where we received a fresh change of clothes and a hot shower. After the shower, all three of us lay down for a long overdue sleep in a real bed. As I tried to sleep, my mind was on Anis and how I wished she was with me to enjoy this moment and how this reminded me of the cargo ship and Jared. This episode had cost the lives of a ship crew and at least eight soldiers and one precious wife. I hope Ron and Tim and the Oman Government realized how very much this had cost me.

Finally, I fell asleep and didn't wake up until late the next day.

It was three weeks before we docked at the port in New Orleans. From there I called Scottie and asked him to come and get us. He was so excited to hear my voice and said he'd leave immediately! Around midnight, Scottie drove up, and what a sight for sore eyes he was! I introduced him to Ron and Tim, and naturally, he wanted to know all about what happened, especially since I had been gone a little over four months.

I told him that there was plenty to tell and that we had a long ride back home, so why not kill two birds with one stone? So all the way back to Texas, I filled him in on everything that happened, especially my relationship with Anis. I emphasized to him the special bond that we shared and how I wasn't sure that I'd ever get over it.

Then Scottie told me about the scuba shop and how he hired two young college students to work part-time. He also told me that he was able to certify the divers for the power company, and they had already called back to schedule another class for additional divers. I jokingly told him it seemed that he didn't need me around.

I could hardly wait to get home to see Fuzzy plus make a trip to east Texas. We pulled into Norton about 9:00 A.M. It was good to be back home and everything seemed to be in order. After giving Fuzzy a little attention, Ron, Tim, and I loaded up in my suburban and headed for Ft. Worth.

After a few hours, we were at Tim's house. What a wonderful reunion it was to see him being reunited with his family who by now had given up any hope of ever seeing him again. After having lunch with them, I left Ron at Tim's house while I headed to east Texas. About mid-afternoon I walked into Robert's office. Janet saw me first and acted like she couldn't believe her eyes. She jumped up from behind her desk and gave me a big family hug while she yelled out to Robert. He was just as thrilled to see me.

Of course, they wanted to know where I had been and how things went. I told them it was a long story and I'd love to sit down and tell them about it. They invited me over to their house for supper, and I told them I'd fill them in on everything then.

I left to go see Uncle Ben, and from his office, I called Mom and Dad. They were so glad to hear from me, and Mom said she had been worried about me because they hadn't heard from me and weren't able to reach me by phone.

She said Scottie had told her I was out of town and she and Dad assumed I was off somewhere in the Caribbean scuba diving, but they thought it was unlike me to go off on a vacation without telling them. I didn't mention to her where I had been and wasn't sure I ever would. I would make that decision later. We chatted a while, and it was so good to hear her voice. I promised to come visit them within a few days.

That night Robert also invited Uncle Ben and Aunt Mary Ann over for supper. As we ate, I told them all that had happened-- how the ship had been raided, our attack on the facility, the rescue, and my relationship with Anis. I couldn't help but tear up as I told them how much I had been looking forward to bringing her to East Texas and introducing her to all the family. I told them how much she was looking forward to coming, and almost before my eyes, those hopes and dreams were gone.

After supper, Janet told me again how thankful they were that I had gotten back home safely. I told her that I was also thankful to be back and that no doubt the Good Lord was looking after me. Then I mentioned to them that I had two more things to do before this chapter in my life could be closed. For one, I needed to get the truth from Kali about who she is and her involvement in all of this, and secondly, I needed to go back and tell Anis' parents what happened to her. They didn't know about the mission and think she is in the United States with me. They need to know the truth about their daughter.

The next morning, after breakfast, I headed to ChemTec to see Kali. This time — I was going to demand answers.

CHAPTER 18

All the way to Ft. Worth, I wondered what I was going to say to Kali, and more importantly, what she was going to say to me. About mid-morning, I walked into the lobby area of ChemTec and asked to speak to Kali. The receptionist called back to her office and was told that she was in a meeting and would not be available until noon. I told the lady at the desk that I'd wait since I had nothing better to do. I grabbed a magazine and settled in a lounge chair over in the corner and waited. I wondered if her meeting was with Ron and Tim.

Finally, it was near noon, and I asked the receptionist if she could check with Kali again, which she did. Soon she came out, and when she saw me, she said, "Hey, Hero! Sounds like mission accomplished! Great job and welcome home!"

"Kali, we need to talk. Can we go someplace for lunch?"

"Sure," she said. "Where would you like to go?"

I didn't care so long as I had some private time with her, so we grabbed a drive-thru burger and went to the park and sat inside the car to eat as it was cold outside.

"Alright, Kali, I'll get straight to the point. Who are you really, and what was your involvement in all of this? Now don't give me the 'just an employee' spill. After what I've gone through, I deserve the truth."

She paused for a short time and said she realized that I had been through a lot and commended the loyalty I had shown to a friend. Then she asked if this was solely for a friend. I assured her that it was, and then I said, "Why did you ask that?"

"I don't know anyone who would do what you did solely for friendship. Sonny Scroggins, you are most definitely one-of-a-kind."

I told her there were several times when I had asked myself the same question – why? But every time I decided to quit and return home, I was stranded and had no way to get home. The plan put forth by Armand kept me there once I "pushed off from the shore."

"Kali, too many things happened that links back to you to be merely coincidental. Now, will you please tell me the truth?"

"Alright, you deserve the truth, but not here. Come over to my apartment tonight at about 7:00, and I'll fill you in. But for now, I need to get back to work. Is that alright with you?"

I agreed to her terms but made sure that I watched my back all afternoon. I didn't trust her and figured she might be bargaining for time to knock me off. I went to a movie theater and sat through the same movie three times just to avoid being out on the street during the afternoon. When it was close to 7:00, I made my way to her apartment. I made sure that I had my pistol with me and that the clip was full of bullets.

I worked up enough courage to knock on her door, and Kali welcomed me and invited me inside. When I walked into her living room, I was surprised to see Armand and Nadir there. "What's going on?" I asked.

Kali asked me to sit down, and Armand took the lead in explaining the mission. He began by saying that neither he nor Nadir represented the Omen Government. "We work for the United States Government and are undercover agents in Yemen. All three of us work for the CIA. It was our government that helped us with all of the arrangements."

I was stunned at what I was hearing. "How does Kali figure into the mix?"

She explained that our government was working on a chemical experiment, but to disguise the real source, they made it appear to be for Omen. None of the people at ChemTec knew any different. As for Tim and Ron, they really thought they were developing a chemical for the nation of Oman.

"Somehow, someone in Yemen found out about it and came and took Tim to develop an antidote. Naturally, we could not involve our government in the rescue nor could we involve the government of Omen because they didn't have any knowledge of what was going on. So you see our dilemma." She said she had been placed within ChemTec as a secret liaison and had gotten close to Ron in order to keep close touch on the progress of the program.

"Once Tim had been taken, we knew where he was because we had embedded a small tracking device inside the leather of his belt. So as long as he had his belt on, we knew where he was. We also did this with Ron, and, yes, Mr. Scroggins, even you."

"Did you slip into my house the Sunday morning after giving me those maps?" I asked.

"Yes, we did," Armand said. "And we implanted tracking devices in the sole of your shoes as well as your belt. We had you in our sights every step of the way until your stay in the ocean. That saltwater did a number on our sensors, and we lost your signal. This is why we were so frantically looking for you in Aden."

Then Kali resumed, "I let a few hints slip to Ron in hopes he had enough care and respect for his comrade that he would solicit some help. What we didn't figure on was someone also grabbing Ron.

However, he had already planted the seed with you before that happened. After that, all I needed to do was fan the flame just a little and drop a few breadcrumbs. Our nation could not allow this kind of military secret falling into the hands of any Middle East country, and you secured our secret. Obviously, we can't reward you for your efforts publicly, but we can compensate you in some way under the table."

I was astounded at what I was hearing and was not sure if I was excited or angry. In one way, I contributed to the welfare of our country, but on the other hand, I felt like I had been used.

"What about Jared?" I asked.

"He was one of us, and we really hated to lose him. We still don't know why his ship was raided. We presume it was someone trying to get to you, but we can't prove that," Nadir answered. "I also had to act surprised when I saw you and you told me that Jared had been killed. Again, he was wearing the devices that allowed us to know where he was at all times."

Then I said, "I need you to make arrangements for me to return to the family of Anis. They think she is in this country with me and has no idea that she has been killed. I owe them the courtesy of telling them what happened and try to help bring closure to them as well as to me."

They said that was a noble and reasonable request and that they would make the arrangements and let me know when they were ready. As we got ready to leave, it was stressed to me that this meeting never happened and that they trusted me to keep all that I was told confidential, and I agreed to do so.

I visited a few days with Mom and Dad before I returned to Norton. About ten days later, I received an envelope in the mail that contained roundtrip airline tickets to Shreveport, Atlanta, and then to Jizan with a note that said, "See Abu when you get there."

Scottie again agreed to run the office, and the next day I made a drive to Shreveport to begin a journey that I dreaded but needed to make. After some twenty hours in the air, I was at the Jizan airport. Once inside, I asked someone in the baggage department for Abu. They pointed to the tarmac. I found the man and told him who I was, and he took me to a helicopter and handed me the keys. I assumed it was for me to use, and I was soon in the air looking for the island where Anis' parents lived. The coast was filled with small islands, and they all looked so much alike that I wasn't sure which island was theirs.

I thought I saw something that looked familiar, so I circled around for a closer look, and sure enough, it was their house. I landed on the nearby beach and said a prayer for wisdom to know what to say to her parents. To complicate things, I would have to communicate the message with sign language.

I mustered enough courage to climb out of the chopper and walked to the house. I was met by Anis' brothers who seemed glad to see me. Then we made our way to the house where I saw her mother. She turned and looked at me with a surprised look and penetrating eyes as if she knew something was wrong. I motioned for her husband, and she sent one of the sons to fetch him.

My heart was racing, and my hands were sweating. Oh how I hated to bear the news that they were about to receive! In a few minutes, all of the family came together. I tried to tell them what happened in sign language but really didn't know where to start. Then I broke down and sobbed like a baby. They obviously sensed that I was hurting. Anis's mother came over and put her hand on my shoulder to console me.

How ironic this was! I came all the way over here to try to console them in the death of their daughter, and now she was trying to console me. Finally, I regained my composure and again tried to explain what happened. I made the motion of someone shooting a rifle. Then I acted like someone getting hit.

Then I heard someone cry out, "Sonny! It's my Sonny!"

I whirled around to see Anis standing at the door! I couldn't believe my eyes nor could I control the tears. Immediately, I rushed over to her and drew her close to me and kissed her.

"Oh Sonny, I thought you were dead!"

"That's funny, because I thought you were dead, and I came to tell your folks what happened to you."

She told me the farmer took her to the hospital where she stayed for several days. When she was released, she made her way back home, but she had no idea what had happened to me. The last thing she knew was that I stayed behind in the mountains to try to slow down the soldiers, and no one had heard from me since.

I assured her that I was alive and well, although I did take a bullet in the shoulder. We spent the rest of the day talking and giggling. This was by far the happiest day of my life. We got in the helicopter and flew to the airport where I made a telephone call to Armand requesting another airline ticket. "Anis is alive, and I'm bringing her home!" He said it would be at the ticket counter tomorrow.

We flew back to the island, and one by one, I flew her family around the island and out over the ocean. Her mom was a little bit scared, but soon relaxed and enjoyed the ride.

That night, Anis and I enjoyed each other's company, and I told her I wanted to take her to a perfect place to spend our honeymoon. With a twinkle in her eye, she asked, "Where?"

"To a secluded cave in the Grand Canyon," I said! "We will have total privacy unless a man that has been bitten by a rattlesnake joins us!" She flashed her beautiful smile and said, "Sounds good to me so long as it is the Grand Canyon in your country!"

I kissed her and said, "You can count on it. I love you so much."